D0144828

The SeaQuel
Les Traveled

LES PENDLETON

Essie Press

Palm Coast Services Inc dba *Essie Press*
901 Sawgrass Court
New Bern, NC 28560
www.essiepress.com
EMAIL: essie-press@lespendleton.com

This book is a work of fiction. The characters, names, incidents, dialogue and plot are the products of the author's imagination or are used fictitiously. Any resemblance to actual persons or events is purely coincidental. Some of the places in the book are real.

ISBN for Print: 978-0-9823358-6-4
         Ebook 978-0-9754740-3-7

Cover by Damonza

Published in the United States of America
February 2015

This book is dedicated to my loving wife and
co-conspirator in my attempts to find adventure, romance and
more time at the helm of our old ketch, *Two Peas*.
Thank you Essie.

Acknowledgments

A big thank you to Betsy Barbeau for her editing work on this novel.

Special thanks to all of our sailing friends who graciously allowed me to use their names, faces, boats and actual experiences in this book. Actual persons gracing the pages of this book are:

Tommy Pollard

Vinny Chianese and Sandy Foster

Frank and Gayle Albertini

Jim and Sara Grimshaw

Jeff Ginn

Michael Keaton

Jim and Vanessa Singer

David and Leigh Pfefferkorn

Lou, Helen, and Chris Schroder

Stuart and Shelia Stovall

1

South Carolina's lowlands were spectacular. They consisted of large fields of wetlands backed up by a thick wall of live oaks. Many of them were draped in Spanish moss and there was an abundance of the one flora that warmed my soul, palms. Actually, there were more palmettos than palm trees, but the fan-like branches waving in the sunlight represented warmth and tropical settings. The day had been beautiful and Essie, Grimshaw and I were down to just our bathing suits, soaking up the long awaited warmth. We were closing in on Florida and, God, were we ready. My bathing suit was nearly worn out, but I felt that if I didn't put it on, Essie might think I was just wanting to observe her fluid movements, encased as she was in a tiny, pink print string bikini. That of course, was my motive exactly.

Grimshaw was proving to be a likable, down-to-earth sort, at least as much as someone out of Hollywood could be. We had stopped in two marinas since leaving Hilton Head. Our primary goal was to dump the holding tank, take on some water and stretch our legs at a local tavern. Both times started innocently enough, but ended with a throng of fans surrounding our table and mobbing Grimshaw. I don't think I could ever enjoy being a celebrity, but he handled it well. I guess, after being in the public eye for over twenty years, he knew it came with the territory. He actually seemed to thrive on the adoration of the fans. It was late in the afternoon. We were poking along down the ICW, each of us with an ice cold Corona and the Gypsy Kings pouring out their Latin rhythms from the cockpit speakers. I turned to Grimshaw.

"Jim, don't the crowds bother you, being constantly after you while you're out in public? It doesn't seem to be upset you at all."

"It took me over fifteen years to get to the point in my career that anyone even recognized me. I wanted to be a successful actor and, now that I'm there, I'm not going to ever be turned off by the things that go along with it. I always thought it was so hypocritical that an actor or anyone in the public eye would say that the crowds bother them, and then drive around in a black stretch limo with dark tinted windows, trying to draw as much attention as they can. Of course, all the time they're bitching about it. It's kind of like a thin woman telling the plastic surgeon, 'I want tits big enough that I'll have to fuss at men for staring at them.' Face it. If they wanted to be left alone, all they'd have to do is drive around in an '84 Chevy with a dent in the fender and dress like normal people. Obscurity is *not* what they're after. Now this, where we are right now, is what life is all about."

"No argument there. I was never much good at anything that produced enough money to feel like I was ahead. That's got to be a good feeling." Essie knew exactly what I was talking about.

"Man, it would be so great to get to the point that I had enough money set aside to not have to worry about it all the time. We could just stay on *Calypso* and keep going. That would be the best life I could possibly imagine."

Grimshaw was undoubtedly used to seeing envy and ours was certainly showing through. "Guys, nothing is ever quite as good as you might think when it comes to work. Making movies is a tough racket. It's a sixteen-hour day, at least six days a week. A lot of it is extremely boring and your entire career hangs in the balance about which movies you choose and then how well the folks that are responsible for the finished product do their work. You can disappear from the business faster than you can appear. Not to mention, even though the pay can be great at times, I've got an agent, a manager, the government, and a litter of ex-wives all sharing quite nicely in my earnings. My fourth and fifth wives were a friggin' bloodbath financially. Don't even let me get started."

"Jim, a lot of us would have a hard time feeling sympathy for you."

Grimshaw put his hand to his brow in his best 'suffering artist' gesture, a well practiced one, I might add. "No one really understands me."

Essie immediately came to his rescue. She bent over, exposing two magnificent orbs that I have already categorized for you as "perky" and hugged him on the neck. "You poor baby. Mommy is here."

Grimshaw, of course, continued to milk it for all it was worth. "At least you, Essie, you truly understand me."

"I do. baby. I do."

"Okay, you snake, unhand my woman."

"That obvious, huh?"

"Pathetic would be a better word."

"Can't blame me for putting forth the effort. You have a beautiful first mate here."

"She is, Jim. She really is."

The conversation was fun and we enjoyed not only each other's company, but the fabulous sunset that was casting a bright orange reflection on the calm water. We continued on until almost dark and then pulled into a small cove just off the side of the

Intracoastal Waterway, known to sailors as the ICW, to spend the night on the hook.

I now watched ever so carefully as we anchored, not wanting a repeat performance of Essie's earlier late-night plunge on which she accompanied the anchor to the bottom. Once the anchor was set, we all grabbed a corner of the cockpit and sat back watching the last rays of light fade away and then the appearance of a bright sliver of moon that would serve as a nightlight for the rest of the evening.

Though we were getting far enough south for the temperatures at night to be moderating, it was still late fall and the sun set quite early, around six p.m. That made for short cruising days and long evenings in the cockpit, enjoying the moment, the music, the Coronas, and each other's company.

Grimshaw had led a very different and fascinating life and loved to have an audience to share his tales with. I particularly enjoyed hearing of his experiences as an officer in the Army and serving as an Army Rangers during the Vietnam War. He had started his acting career as the Military Technical Advisor for "Magnum PI" starring Tom Selleck. He was stationed in Hawaii and that's where the show was filmed. He had wanted to act since high school and this opportunity gave him the chance to start getting small parts while serving as a technical advisor. This was at the end of his twenty-plus year military career and he could think of no better way to spend the rest of his work life. He had achieved a great deal of success as a character actor but never quite hit the major star category that all actors shoot for. Still, he was at peace with what he had accomplished.

Grimshaw and Cappy

We were engrossed in conversation and enjoying the surreal quietness of the anchorage when an approaching rumble could be heard in the distance. My first thought was that it was a low flying helicopter but the sound wasn't quite correct. As it grew louder, it sounded more like the engine of a stock car at the Charlotte Motor Speedway, but that was out of the question. It had to be some sort of boat, but the engines were straining too hard to be coming down a pitch-black waterway at a high rate of speed. The noise became more definable; it was one I had heard before. The Fountain Boats Company was in Little Washington, North Carolina, and their engine's sound was pretty damn unique. It was a cross between race-car and helicopter, so we were right on all counts. We stared down the waterway looking for the approach of running lights but even as the sound grew very loud, none were visible.

It was at that moment a vessel went screaming past *Calypso* at what must have been sixty miles, or maybe eighty miles an hour. It not only had no lights visible, but was so dark that we could barely make out its blurred shape as it passed. The hull was undoubtedly painted a dark color. I had experienced this one time before, many years earlier, and I came to the same conclusion then as now. There could only be one reason for running at night, in the dark at a high rate of speed – running drugs. We were in a fairly remote area with a shallow inlet. That would let an extremely shoal-draft, high-speed boat capable of going offshore either meet a large boat forty or fifty miles out or recover a package dropped from a plane at low altitude. With the help of night vision goggles, they could run wide open down the ICW and be in port before anyone was the wiser. Only a moment later, the night was quiet and dark again.

"What was that? Did you hear it? Sounded like someone yelling."

"You're right. It sounds like somebody's in the water."

I went below and grabbed a high powered spotlight. After scanning the dark waters for a couple of minutes, we all saw splashes and a person in the water about a hundred yards south of our position. With Jim's help I lowered the dinghy as fast as possible.

"I hope this old outboard starts. I haven't used it in quite a while."

After a few pulls the rusty three horsepower motor fired up. Essie tossed the line holding us to *Calypso* and Jim and I took off. She held the spotlight focused on the area where we had seen the person in the water. I pushed the dinghy as fast as the small motor would power it.

"There he is!" Jim followed the beam of light to what was clearly someone having trouble staying afloat.

I steered toward the nearly drowned individual and pulled alongside. Jim and I each grabbed an arm and struggled to pull him into the inflatable Zodiac. Trying to bring someone out of the water and onto a dinghy can be a very tricky maneuver and could easily result in everyone going into the water. The process took over five minutes and was physically draining. By the time we had him on board, we were all soaked and the dink had four inches of water in the bottom. The man lay on the floor of the boat panting like a retriever who'd just brought back a duck from the center of the Chesapeake Bay. He was breathing on his own and didn't seem to be in any immediate trouble other than out of breath. I cranked the motor again and we headed back to *Calypso*, without the urgency that had accompanied us previously. We came alongside and with a great deal of pushing and pulling we finally got the man aboard. He sat down in the cockpit and spoke for the first time, still breathing heavily as he spoke.

"Thanks, guys. I was a goner, a dead fish floating on the ocean if you hadn't shown up."

Jim corrected him. "Actually, you're not in the ocean, just the ICW, the Intracoastal Waterway."

"Oh that's just great. I'm sure there are friggin' alligators in here everywhere, am I right? Either way, without you guys I was a dead man. I owe you guys."

As he spoke he started to scan the horizon as if looking for someone other than *Calypso* and her crew. On some sort of cue, he became a little more guarded in what he was saying. We all felt it. "Any other boats around?" He did a three sixty as he asked the question.

"Nope. The only other boat we've seen came roaring through here with no lights on just before we heard you."

"Bastards. They tossed me in the drink."

We were all a little incredulous at the remark. "They threw you overboard?"

"Affirmative. They knew I couldn't swim and I'm guessing they didn't notice you folks over here. Oh yeah, I'm Vinny, Vincent Chianese to be precise. Who are you guys?" He noticed Essie. "I'm sorry, and gals."

"I'm Les, this is Essie and Jim. If you don't swim, then you're lucky we were anchored here."

"You're telling me. Two more minutes and it would have been all over. Do you have a towel I could borrow? I'm starting to get cold."

"I'm sorry. I'll go down and see if we don't have some dry clothes as well," Essie said as she started to go below.

I asked the question we all had on the tips of our tongues. "Why did they throw you over? I'm mean that would have been murder. That's about as serious as it gets."

"Well, to tell you the truth, this is all about a business deal that went south. I had introduced the folks in the boat you saw to some associates of mine from out of the country. They commenced to set up the purchase of some rare artifacts from South America from them. I was supposed to get a…well, a finder's fee that was a decent chunk of bread. I guess they decided to keep my share and let me swim back to Ohio."

Jim was not too guarded in his comments. "Sounds a lot like a drug deal that went sour."

Vinny was taken aback by Jim's bluntness. "I'm not sure just what it was they were purchasing; I just introduced everyone. Get my drift?"

"Yeah, and I gotta tell you, you don't 'drift' all that well."

"Funny, that's funny."

Essie returned with some dry clothes and a towel. Vinny stepped to the back deck, dried off and returned looking a lot more presentable. He could best be described as a cross between Joe Pesci and Ernest Hemingway. He was about five two, two hundred fifty pounds with a salt and pepper beard. His accent was decidedly northern with a large Italian flavor. Essie reappeared with a steaming cup of coffee, of which he made short work.

"I wonder if you've got something down below I could eat; I'm starving. And how about something a little stronger to warm me up?"

"How about a Corona?"

"I was thinking a little harder than that."

Jim offered his private stash. "I've got some brandy."

"Perfect. Looks like I wound up in the right place."

"You're lucky you wound up anyplace."

My sense of survival dictated that I ask him, "Do you think you're 'associates' will be coming back through here? I don't think I want to meet them."

"Naw, they'll be onboard a private plane headed back to New Jersey within the hour. I'm sure they think I'm sleeping with the fishes."

Vinny's descriptive analogy from "The Godfather" seemed very natural. It was apparent we had netted a "family" member. My immediate concern was how to get him off *Calypso* and not associated with us as fast as possible. He was someone that could undoubtedly attract a lot of attention that we didn't need or want. We had a few more beers as the evening wore on. Vinny turned out to be an amiable sort with a funny story or two on every imaginable topic. He and Grimshaw exchanged jokes until all of our cheeks were sore from laughing. We carried on until about midnight and then turned in. The night was quiet; *Calypso* bobbed on her anchor gently until the sun broke through the ports the next morning.

Vinny - Fresh from his "swim"

Dawn near an inlet is a noisy and bouncy situation as sport fishing boats race at dawn to their favorite fishing holes offshore. Essie had fixed coffee and toast for everyone, but drinking it without wearing it proved to be a daunting task. There was a boat wake to deal with every few minutes.

"So, Vinny, what do you want us to do with you?"

"Where are you guys headed?"

"I would guess that unless we make an unplanned stop at some hole in the wall marina, the next place we'll be going ashore is St. Augustine."

"Florida?"

"That's right. It's just a little bit over the State line. We'll be there tomorrow evening. You're welcome to join us that far."

"Count me in. Believe me, after yesterday, nobody's expecting me any time soon."

We sat in the cockpit and watched the sun rise. Vinny stared at Grimshaw and asked, "Do I know you? You look like somebody I should know."

Grimshaw gave his best I'm-used-to-this-I get-this-all-the-time smile and facetiously replied: "You probably know my face from the hundred or so movies I've been in, I'm a pretty big film star."

Vinny responded without any consideration of Grimshaw's statement. "Naw, that ain't it. You ever been in the pen?"

"You mean prison?"

"Yeah, the big house, the hoosegow, whatever."

"Well, I spent a night or two in the brig during my years in Army. Never in 'the big house.'"

"Okay, but I'm sure I know you from somewhere. It'll come to me. Movie star, huh? That's a good one."

This was the hottest morning we had spent so far. In fact, it was comparable to a mid-summer day in August. There was almost no perceptible wind and we sweltered as noon approached. We stayed huddled under the bimini for protection from the intense sun. We motored along still towing the dinghy used to pull Vinny out of the water the previous evening. The surface of the water looked like an oily mirror. We were all relieved when a breeze finally started to fill in. However, it was only a short while later that dark clouds began to move with the wind in our direction. In the center of the clouds it was easy to pick out intense stripes of lightning. I had been through a lot of thunderstorms over the years and knew the best precaution was to get prepared the moment you hear thunder.

"Let's get *Calypso* prepared for a blow. We'll need to make sure the sails are secured and I'll get the anchor ready to drop if the storm gets closer to us."

My normal strategy was to secure the sails and anything loose on deck, drop the anchor, set it, and leave the motor running in neutral in case the anchor started to slip. We undertook all of those precautions and watched as the sky turned dark green. Past experience had also shown me that the worst storms were accompanied by a greenish sky and not the normal dark gray to black of a run-of-the-mill thunderstorm. This one was going to be strong. Within five minutes the wind picked up to about eighteen to twenty knots and the cracks of thunder were getting very loud. As I scanned the water ahead, the telltale signs of strong winds were apparent causing the water to get irritated and dark.

"Here it comes, everybody needs to get where they want to be when it hits. Either go below or stay in the cockpit. Above all, don't touch anything attached to the mast and nothing metal if you can avoid it. I'm serious."

I could see concern on Essie's face. She looked at the three crewmates with her and marveled at the apparent calm on our faces. "Aren't you guys worried? This looks like a pretty bad storm to me."

Grimshaw replied, "It doesn't look nearly as scary as tracers coming at me in the night during a firefight in Nam. Now that's scary."

Vinny smiled and added, "Essie, is there beer handy? Tell me where they are and I'll get it myself."

Not wanting glass in the cockpit when the weather was about to get rough, I countered, "Essie, just pour one into a plastic cup and hand it to Vinny. You want one, Jim?"

"Why not? I'm certainly hot enough and I don't want to meet Davy Jones without a trace of alcohol in my system."

Essie shook her head at the two of them as she went to pour the drinks. "Might as well get me one too, Essie. Jim's reasoning makes sense."

We all sat back in the cockpit as the swells began to build. As we were in the Intracoastal Waterway, the waves would never get much over two feet so the concern was primarily for the lightning and wind. Since we had taken the proper precautions, I was comfortable with the situation. At least as comfortable as possible, sitting on the floating ground platform of a fifty-foot lightning rod. There was no buildup. A blast of air came across the water so fast it was like being run over by a freight train.

"Good God, Les! This is like a hurricane."

"I think the winds are well over hurricane force, Jim. I'd bet around ninety miles per hour."

We had to practically scream to hear each other speak.

Calypso lined up with the wind on her bow and pulled hard on the anchor chain. I looked toward shore and it was obvious that the anchor was slipping. The diesel was still running in neutral so I asked Jim and Vinny to go forward and let out some more anchor rode as I put the engine in gear and moved forward. This would give them some slack on the line. Otherwise, it was so tight they couldn't have gotten it off the cleat. The waves were now very large to be in a small sound with an average depth of less than ten feet. As I moved forward I heard and felt an object striking the stern of the boat. I knew with one quick look what happened. We were still towing the dinghy with a short rope called a painter, which was used to secure it to *Calypso*. We had crested a wave and the dinghy had surfed forward and under the stern. The painter was long enough that it had been sucked onto the prop of *Calypso,* instantly bringing her to a stop as the fouled propeller shaft could turn no further. It took only a second or so for the full effect of the situation to become apparent. The dinghy was now trapped under our stern and every time *Calypso* came off a wave she would slap down on the dinghy with a painful crashing sound.

"We're either going to punch a hole in the bottom of *Calypso* or sink the dinghy."

Essie added, "It looks like we're still dragging anchor too. We'll be on bottom soon if we can't reset it. What do we need to do?"

The answers didn't sound like a lot of fun.

"First, hand me a dock line. I'll tie it around the seat of the dinghy so that I can cut the other painter free. The dink will swing out from under us. Essie, go below and get me a steak knife so I can cut it. Be careful and don't fall with it in your hand. We're bouncing pretty bad right now."

In just seconds Essie was back. I took the knife and climbed down the stern of the boat onto the swim ladder. It was basically a small stainless steel, three-step ladder mounted to the stern of the boat for boarding after swimming. As each wave ran under *Calypso*, she pounded back down on the dinghy and I was more than a little terrified at the prospect of holding the knife in one hand, while leaning away from the boat balancing on the tiny steps. If the two boats didn't crush me between them, there was a good chance I'd cut my hand off. I could see real concern on Essie's face.

"Please, baby, be careful. I don't like you doing this."

"Then we're together on that, but I don't have a choice or we'll be sitting in a sinking boat very shortly."

After a few passes against the painter, the line finally sheared under the blade and the dinghy came free from under the boat.

"Essie, try to start the motor. Don't grind it; just see if it will fire."

A quick turn of the ignition convinced me that the prop shaft still had a lot of the dinghy painter wrapped around it and it was not going to start until it was removed.

"Okay, for my next trick, I'm going to have to get in the water and cut the rope off the shaft."

Now I could see concern on everyone's face.

"Babe, can you get me my swimsuit? God, I don't want to do this. The water is cold as crap, and the depth finder was showing only seven feet of water."

Vinny asked the obvious. "Is that bad? For my taste, shallower is better. Two less feet of water and we can stand on the bottom."

"This boat is our home, our only home. I can do this. When it's this shallow, as she comes off a wave my feet will hit the muddy bottom and not barnacles I'm praying. And when it rises up, it'll lift me clean out of the water."

I put the bathing suit on and moved back to the stern of the boat again. Grimshaw came over with another dock line.

"Here, tie this to your waist. At least if you kill yourself, we can bring your body back aboard."

"Right, right, And you can comfort Miss Essie, am I right?"

"For you, Les, just for you. Captain, my captain."

I tied the line around my waist. "Thanks. Now I know I'll make it back." I eased off the stern. It was still blowing hard, raining, and lightning was crackling every few seconds. I jumped off the stern. Within a second after I hopped in I started to appreciate the line around my waist. Without it I would have been blown away from the boat immediately.

"Pull me back to the stern." Vinny and Grimshaw pulled on the dock line until I was virtually under the back of the boat. It was rising up and then slamming down with enough force to crush my skull if my timing was off even a little. I waited until it started its move upward, took a deep breath and lunged under the boat grabbing the shaft as it went past me. The visibility was literally nothing. This would be a 'by feel only' operation. It was a bit disconcerting that I couldn't see through the water but about every ten seconds I could hear thunder and the water got visibly lighter as if a searchlight was being shined around me. I could feel the rope around the shaft and under my hand. The boat fell back into the water and just as I predicted, pushed me to the muddy bottom. My legs went a full two feet into the slimy muck. Knowing I couldn't hold my breath long and sustain much of this pounding, I started to take my free hand and saw away at the line around the shaft. It didn't want to come free. The boat rose out of the water again and again. Each time I'd suck in as large a gasp of air as I could and prepare to be shoved back under and into the mud. If there was anything on the bottom, from a tree stump to an oyster bed, I would be in trouble. After what seemed an eternity, the cut pieces of line began to break free. I pulled at them until I could feel the shaft was free of the line. Completely spent I let go of the shaft and let my weight pull me out with the line tied to my waist keeping me behind *Calypso*.

"Okay, get me onboard. You're going to have to help me up. I'm shot."

Vinny and Jim leaned over the stern and with a great deal of exertion managed to get me back aboard. I lay in the cockpit floor for at least five minutes before I spoke. "Essie, see if the engine will start."

Essie turned the key and miraculously the motor fired right up. "Thank God."

I stood up, took the wheel and started forward once more.

"Let's try this again. As I get you some slack on the anchor rode, let out about fifty more feet of line and cleat her off."

"Aye, aye, captain."

The increase in rode allowed the anchor to set and this time she held. We all gathered back in the cockpit and passed some dry towels around. With our drenched swim trunks and flowered towels around our soaked bodies, Grimshaw and I looked like a pair of old Samoan pearl divers after a hard day at work. Vinny looked over at us and inquired.

"How much longer 'til you can get me to shore? I think it's becoming pretty clear to me that I'm not a water person. I'm thinking a plate of hot lasagna, some Sinatra music, and a nice ride home with my old lady in our Porsche Boxter."

Grimshaw, dripping wet and looking as disheveled as I was, looked over at Vinny and tried one last time.

"Reminds me of the time I was filming a movie with Mel Gibson…"

Without pausing for a breath Vinny replied, "Grimshaw, you're so full of it. Movie star, that's a too much. How much longer 'til we're at the marina?"

"Tomorrow, Vinny, lunchtime. How about a beer?"

The rain finally stopped, and the sun came back out hotter than ever. We motored down the ICW at six knots, with the Florida Keys on our mind. We crossed into Florida and Essie let out a cheer as we saw the Welcome to Florida sign along the shore. We continued until the sun disappeared. After such a long and tiring day, we anchored once more and then turned in early.

Undoubtedly fueled with the excitement of finally being in Florida, we rose again with the sun. I helped Essie get the coffee going and she warmed up some bagels. Grimshaw and Vinny joined us in the cockpit for a quick bite before we weighed anchor.

"We did it, Cappy! We're in the tropics. I think this is just the start of a wonderful and warm winter. I've been dreaming about this for years."

"I know, Essie. This is what I've been thinking about for most of my life. Palm trees, clear water, and warm winter days."

2

We were nearing St. Augustine, the ancient town in northeast Florida thought to be the oldest continuous settlement in North America. I had driven through the town before and was impressed with the Lion's Bridge that spanned the main anchorage. I also remembered the town as beautiful. Essie had never seen it, so I was excited to be with her to see it for the first time. We would need to spend at least one night at a local marina to fuel up, empty our holding tank, take on some water and get rid of our trash. It was just as the skyline started to reveal the bridge that I heard the most terrifying words a captain can hear. They came from Grimshaw.

"Hey, Cappy, how about letting me take her in? You know I can handle her pretty damn good now."

My common sense kept saying, "No, fool, don't do it." No one was more surprised than me when I said, "If you really feel like you have her under control..."

"I know I can do it, if you guys will just help me with the lines."

I could see a marina with a large restaurant about two hundred yards past the Lion's Bridge.

"Okay, Jim, that's where we want to go. Looks like they have a fuel pump at the end of the dock closest to us. I'll give them a call."

I retrieved the marina information from the Waterway Guide and hailed them on the VHF. They were prompt to respond and very professional.

"Okay, skipper. We'll be standing at the end of the dock ready to take your lines. I'll be wearing a yellow shirt and wave to you as you approach."

"Affirmative. We'll be there in just a couple of minutes."

Grimshaw had *Calypso* moving slowly toward the dock and the angle of approach appeared to be fine. Essie took a dock line, secured it to bow cleat and stood by to throw it to the marina attendant when we were close enough. Vinny held one on the stern. I stayed on the deck just behind the cockpit to be certain that Grimshaw was handling things correctly.

"That's it, Jim. Easy now."

A tugboat captain I knew always told me to never approach anything faster than I was willing to hit it. Those words flashed through my mind at just that moment.

"Jim, we're getting close, put her in neutral. Let's back her down so we just coast up to the dock. Neutral, put her in neutral."

There's a handle on either side of *Calypso*'s steering wheel pedestal. On the starboard is the fuel control and the gearshift is on the port. Grimshaw correctly grabbed the gearshift lever and pulled back on it to the neutral position so the boat would slow down. As we slowed to a speed that would not counter the current yet maintain proper steerage, I requested him to push the lever and put the engine back in forward. I guess it was just from the lack of experience that Grimshaw pushed the fuel lever and not the gear shift.

"No Jim, not the fuel; the other shifter."

Without pulling the fuel control lever back to slow the engine speed, he quickly pushed the gearshift lever into forward. *Calypso* lurched forward at the exact moment that she should have been coming to a stop at the dock. I could see the panic on the dockhand's face as our boat slammed into the floating dock and rose up at least a foot onto the dock's surface. I jumped into the cockpit, pushed the gearshift back into the neutral and turned the fuel lever back to idle. We slid back into the water. It did not take a scientist to guess that we had caused some damage to the dock and maybe to our own hull.

"Oh man, Les. I'm sorry. I don't know what happened. I thought I had it under control."

"It's my fault, Jim. I'm the captain here; it's my fault. Don't worry about it."

Meanwhile, Essie and Vinny had thrown their lines to the dockhand and we were secured to the dock we had just rammed. I know my face was blood red with embarrassment as I jumped down on the dock and went over to the attendant. "How much damage did we do?"

"I've seen worse, Skipper. It's not all that much, but anything is expensive when you're talking about dock work. It looks to me like you've broken a couple of planks at the least. We'll have to lift them off to see if the Styrofoam blocks underneath have been damaged. You're probably looking at a couple thousand bucks worth, I hate to tell you. You do have insurance, don't you?"

"Well, to be truthful with you, no. But I do have some cash and I'll cover whatever the damages are. We can't afford to stay here a long time though. We were only going to stay for one night after we fueled up so, if you could find out what the repairs will cost, I'd like to go ahead and straighten up with you today."

"I'll try to get the dock guy out here today. Meanwhile, you want to top off the fuel?"

"Yes, and water. Then I'd like a slip for the night."

"That's fine, Captain. I'm sorry about your misfortune today, but that's boating, ain't it?"

"You're right. That's boating."

By early evening *Calypso* was tucked into a slip. There was virtually no damage to her bow, just a few small scratches that could easily be buffed out with a little rubbing compound and wax. We walked the short distance to a small restaurant in the heart of the tourist district. St. Augustine is a charming historic city on the water. There were horse-drawn carriages taking folks on tours of the town. We could see the old Spanish Fort just a block down the street. There were a lot of tourists everywhere. The restaurant was more of a deli. We were drawn to it by the sounds of steel drum music coming from the speakers by the door. Within thirty minutes we were all well into our third drink and engaged in embellishing the events of the past two days. I could see that the lightning storm tale was going to be a winner and undoubtedly get much more exciting as time passed. Jim was particularly contrite about the docking episode.

"Cappy, I swear I thought I had it under control. I feel terrible."

"Don't worry about it. Every docking on a sailboat is a controlled crash at best. We all walked away from it with no broken bones. I'm just glad to be here."

"What about the dock? Aren't they going to want you to fix it for them? If you let me know what it costs I'll be glad to have my agent send you a check. I don't really have it with me. Don't ever carry much serious cash as I have a bad habit of spending whatever I have."

"Me too, except I've spent whatever I had on me. That's not happening much anymore. We still have a little traveling kitty thanks to a benefactor that wanted us to be able to continue our journey. We'll be okay."

Essie slid over beside me and was gently rubbing my back as she sipped on her Cosmo.

"What are you going to do now, Vinny? We got you to shore like we said we would. Do we need to be looking over our shoulders for your 'friends'?"

"This would be the last place anybody would expect to find me. You're safe. Besides, most of my friends 'love me.' As a matter of fact, some of my real friends back home will be very perturbed with the folks that took me swimming. They'll have a really rough time explaining how that happened. I'm sure they've already told our mutual friends that they haven't seen me since they dropped me off at some marina down here. It should be interesting. I guess I'll just stay tonight aboard with you folks if you'll be kind enough to let me. Tomorrow I'll rent a car and drive home."

"You're certainly welcome to stay aboard tonight."

Vinny looked over at Grimshaw. "What about you, Marlon Brando? I guess it's back to Hollywood for premieres and cocktail parties in Beverly Hills?"

"I've done some of that, but that's generally not me. I've got to go see a woman in Fort Lauderdale and then it's back to the real world. You know, working at Starbucks in Los Angeles."

"I thought so. Movie star, my ass." Vinny slapped Jim on the back. "Whatever you do buddy, you're all right. You ever need somebody to watch your back or bail you out of a tight spot, you call old Vinny and I'm there. You too, Cappy and Miss Essie. You've made a good friend here. I owe you and I don't ever run from a debt. I'll give you a phone number and you call me if you need anything. Anything. You got it?"

We both smiled, knowing it would be a very long shot that we'd ever see this interesting little guy again. "We got you, Vinny.

Let's get another round and then head on back to *Calypso*. I'm starting to wear down."

Two young girls walked up to our table. "Mr. Grimshaw, could we take our picture with you?"

Jim looked over at Vinny and winked. "It would be an honor. Cappy, you want to work the camera while I hug these young ladies?" He put an arm behind each of them and they all smiled for the camera. I took several shots as I was never that good with photographs. The girls each gave Jim a quick peck on the cheek and walked off bubbling with excitement.

Vinny looked over at Jim. "Okay, wiseguy, what do you really do? Seriously."

We laughed and told a few more lies before heading back. The evening was cool and as we walked, we embraced the spectacular views everywhere around us. The soft yellow lights peering out the shuttered windows of the old colonial homes and tourist hangouts that dotted the waterfront reflected off the pristine waters that touched the other side of the main road along its entire length. The anchor lights of all the sailboats in the harbor added to the reflections. This was a beautiful place we were in. Essie and I held hands like school kids as we walked with our new friends back to our floating piece of heaven.

Things had been going too well I guess. That was about to be corrected. The marina's dock master came to us early the next morning with the bad news about the dock. It would cost twenty-six hundred bucks to put her back like she was before our visit. I had no choice but to go back to our peanut jar and get him the money. I did get a receipt. If I ever made enough money to pay taxes again, maybe I could write it off somehow. Essie knew I was upset and, as usual, offered the comfort and concern I needed at just the right moment.

"It's only money. What we have is so much more important than that. We'll just keep going and you'll never miss it. How much do we have left?"

"We're probably all right for a while; there's about twelve grand still in the treasury. You're right, as long as you're willing to hang with me, nothing's going to ruin it."

Boy did I speak too quickly. We went back to *Calypso* and prepared to get underway. I had fired up the diesel and Essie had taken the last bag of trash to the marina's dumpster. As she made her way back along the floating dock, she was followed by two Sheriff's deputies. I could see from the direction they were looking, we were the target of their search. Essie came aboard and they approached us from alongside the dock.

"We'd like to speak with Les Pendleton if he's aboard."

"That would be me. I want you to know that I've already settled up with the dock master for the damages and he indicated there were no further issues. What's the problem?"

"Don't know what you're talking about, Mr. Pendleton. We're here to serve papers on you and impound this vessel."

"You're what? Why would you want to impound my boat?"

"There's a court order to impound this vessel until the judge's ruling on your divorce determines how the proceeds from its sale will be divided between you and your estranged spouse. That's all this order says on it. I'm very sorry, sir, but you're going to need to get your personal items and vacate while we're here."

"I can't believe this. I gave her the home, the cars, the furniture, all our savings, the cash in the bank, and now she wants the only thing that means anything to me."

Essie came up beside me and read the order.

"That's why she wants it gone, baby. Hell hath no fury like a woman scorned."

"Scorned? She didn't want me while I was there and now that I'm gone she still wants to ruin me."

"We'll get through this, baby. There's more boats than this one out there."

I walked back over to the closest deputy. "What will they do with the boat? Will they take it back to North Carolina?"

"Don't know. They might order it sold right here and have the proceeds sent to the court for distribution."

"Distribution, my ass. To give to my ex is what you mean."

"I'm sorry, sir, but that's not really any of our concern. We just process the papers because that's what they pay us to do. I can tell you that if you hope to get any of the proceeds out of the boat, you better make arrangements with the marina for dockage here until the issue is resolved. Otherwise, they can put a lien on the boat for the court to pay them out of the proceeds prior to distribution."

"Thanks. That's great news. I can now pay the slip rent I couldn't afford to pay while I was living on the boat so that the court can sell the boat and give the money to my ex-wife. What a great deal that is. I can't believe this. I knew things were going too good."

Essie tightened her grip around my waist. "Come on, baby. Let's get our stuff. I'll tell Jim and Vinny so they can clear out too."

Almost on cue, it started to rain.

"Essie, I'll go talk to the dock master about storing *Calypso* for a while. Maybe I can make a deal with the court to keep her and I don't want the marina claiming her before I find out what the story is."

Essie was waiting on the dock with all our luggage, what little there was, beside her on the dock.

"Well, Cappy, what's the verdict?"

"I had always heard that keeping a boat in a marina in Florida was for rich people."

"The verdict?"

"We are now twenty seven hundred bucks lighter."

"Good Lord! You'd be better off to just let the court have her."

"With my luck they'll let her sit here 'til the marina owns her and then bill me for thousands more."

"We'll work this out, baby. Don't you worry about it. You and I will handle this together. We'll find a way."

Jim and Vinny came up the dock. Jim had his bag and Vinny had just the clothes he was wearing when we plucked him out of the water. "What's happening, Cappy?"

"I'm officially without a boat. My wife's attorney wants the boat impounded 'til it can be sold and then give her the money. I'm sure I'll get nothing but bills out of any of this. So, I'm back to ground zero. I've got just what I was born with and a gym bag with a hundred bucks worth of clothes and shaving cream."

Essie, ever positive, responded, "And me. As long as we have each other, we don't need anything else. We're going to be just fine. Everything else is just stuff. You'll see."

Jim and Vinny were genuinely touched.

"That's a tough break man. I know how much you loved that old boat. Hell, I loved it."

Vinny immediately wanted to take a different approach. "Les, I can make that boat disappear overnight. A new paint job, a new title and you're back in business."

"Vinny, I don't doubt you could and don't think I don't appreciate the offer, but I'd always be looking over my shoulder. Besides, until I get this divorce worked out, my life is not my own. I guess we need to go back to North Carolina and get this crap over with. Then I'll take Essie here and we'll follow our dreams wherever they go without looking back."

"Okay, man, but don't forget I'm always here if you need a little help and you don't know where to turn. Vinny don't forget a friend."

The afternoon was interesting. First, a Bell Ranger helicopter landed next to the marina and picked up Grimshaw. He was a great guy and if I hadn't been holding Essie's waist real tight, I think he'd have taken her with him. Hell, he tried anyway. I just felt as he flew off to wonderland that we'd cross paths again. Vinny was still there and making his services available.

"Look, Cappy, I've got to rent a car and get going. How about you and Essie keeping me company as far as Carolina? I'll drop you off wherever you want."

"That sounds like a good offer, Vinny. We'll take you up on that."

Vinny placed a collect call to someplace called Sardinia Imports and told them to send him a car, his 'usual.' About ten minutes later a new black Mercedes 500 pulled up to the marina and asked for Vinny.

"Let's go, guys. Our wheels are here."

"Let me go take just one more look at my boat."

Essie walked with me down to the dock. I'm not an overly emotional person but I have to admit to a tear as I looked at my sanctuary sitting there, soon to be taken to the auction block, never to share any more adventures with me.

"Goodbye, old girl. Good luck. I'll miss you."

"Baby, I told you. Everything works out the way it's supposed to. We're not in charge of the schedule and we don't even know what's best for us. You just have to trust that this will all work out for the best. I know it will. Come on now. Give me a little hug."

I embraced Essie and could feel the love pour from her every touch. I knew if nothing else in my life was right at the moment, she was. "Okay, Essie. Let's get on with it."

As we approached the car, Vinny held the door open for us. Essie volunteered to sit in the back so that the 'guys' could talk. Interstate 95 was only a short distance from town. Within minutes we were headed back north at about eighty miles per hour.

"Make you nervous, Cappy?"

"I gotta tell you, when I drive, I'm the old fart that everyone is flying by while flipping me the bird. I hate the highways. I guess that's what I love so much about cruising on a sailboat; sometimes the harbors are crowded but when you're underway, you pretty much have the sea to yourself."

"I'll probably think differently about boats after the last couple of days with you guys."

As the hours wore on, the three of us related to each other how we got where we were in our lives, in a nutshell of course.

As it turned out, Vinny grew up in Ohio where his old man ran a filling station and garage. He learned about cars and motors early on and had been a sports car aficionado all his life. Mercedes had become his car of choice as he got older because his back couldn't handle the hard suspension of a Porsche or a Corvette. He had been a service manager of a Porsche dealership at one time, along with being a sales manager for a construction company and numerous other stints at different jobs. I was more than a little surprised that his history had no mention of working for The Family. I was certain that someone in his family had the first name of Don.

I could hardly believe it when he said he was now married to a much younger woman who had her PhD in stem cell research and was the head of development for a super tech firm. I found that a hard match to visualize. I could much easier see him with Betty Rizzo, the Stockard Channing character in "Grease." But I had learned long ago not to make assumptions about people, so I just took it all in stride. Finally, I felt he was candid enough that I could broach the subject that was on my mind ever since we first fished him out of the water.

"Vinny, based on how we met you, I have to ask you..."

"Go ahead; ask me anything."

"You say you work for a company that handles recalls for car manufacturers out of Detroit."

"That's right."

"Well, what's with these unsavory 'associates' that threw you in the water and left you to drown? I gotta tell you, after what we saw, and you told us, I would have bet you were in the mob, you know, the mafia."

"There's no such thing as the mafia. The cops just made that crap up so they could raise your taxes and hire a lot of guys to spend more money. It's all bullshit."

"What about guys like John Gotti and Meyer Lansky? How about Bugsy Siegel?"

"Ben. Ben Siegel. He hated the nickname. He wacked some guys for calling him that."

"How do you know all this?"

"I saw Warren Beatty in 'Bugsy.'" Great flick. But the mob ain't real. There's just a lot of Italians up in my area and when times got tough, some of them turned to heisting joints to pay their bills. But it was never an organized group of super criminals or anything like that."

"That's pretty hard to believe, Vinny. I heard about the Costa Nostra and the Mafia all my life. There's been books and movies and documentaries about their lives. What about 'The Godfather'?"

"Bullshit, all bullshit. Never happened."

"Damn, that's wild. But I guess you'd know." I still knew there was a mob but I wasn't going to belabor the point with him.

"Of course, all that being said, Cappy, if there ever comes a time when you need a little muscle, er, help, and you didn't know who to call, you got my number. I know some guys, actually a lot of guys, all over the place that I can call and get a favor when I need one. They're not organized crime guys or anything like that. They're just good friends that I work with on and off. They'll do just about anything I need to have done. You know those guys who threw me overboard and left me to drown, right?"

"Of course."

"In a strange twist of fate, one of 'em's house blew up cause of a propane leak last night."

"You're kidding?"

"Gospel truth. And if that weren't a strange enough coincidence, one of the other guys was parking his plane in a hangar in Jersey and it blew up too."

"How?"

"Propane leak."

"That's a little too much coincidence, Vinny."

"Think so?"

"I always heard that good karma attracts good people to you and bad karma attracts bad things. They must have had a lot of bad karma. And I'm told that the third guy who was with them felt so bad about everything that he went to my brother's house and dropped off a bag with all the money they made on that deal."

"The money they made selling the rare South American artifacts?"

"Yeah."

By seven p.m. we were in New Bern. Vinny had kept us awake and laughing most of the way. "Okay, guys. As bad as I hate to call this party to a close, I need you to drop me off at the airport in New Bern. You know where it is?"

"Sure, it sits right on the side of the river, almost downtown. Is there a flight leaving this late you can catch?"

"Absolutely. Drive me to the General Aviation terminal."

"You mean the area for private planes?"

"Yeah, a buddy is going to pick me up. He's got a small plane. And there he is, sitting right by the truck out there getting fueled."

"That's a Cessna Citation. That's one of the sexiest private jets there is."

"It's nice, Cappy. We use it quite a bit."

"I guess the recall business must be pretty lucrative."

"It's his plane. He just gives me a ride when he has the time. Come on, I'll introduce you to him."

We drove up next to the fenced-in private aircraft area. Vinny waved to the guy standing by the plane and we walked through the security gate without so much as a question from the armed guard stationed there.

"Hey, Tank, here's some folks I want you to meet. This is Cappy and Essie. They saved my ass from drowning when our friends from Columbia deposited me in the drink. I owe them big time. They're salt of the earth kind of people."

The guy looked like an Italian TV wrestler. He was large and dark but had a very engaging smile. He held out both hands and grabbed Essie's and mine at the same time. "Hey, you saved my buddy Vinny's life. You're on my A list. You ever need anything, you let Vinny know and I'm there. You ever need a plane, a car, whatever, I'm here for you. We don't forget our friends. Read me?"

"I think so. It's nice to meet you, Tank. So this jet is yours, huh?"

"Not hardly. Belongs to Frank, the guy we all work for. We get to use it when we need it for the most part. Sure beats the hell out of the airlines, what with their security and all. I take being frisked personally. Okay. Well Vincent, I'm all fueled up and there's a front headed to Jersey later this evening with some pretty strong winds I'm told. So we better put the pedal to the metal. I'll have us home in an hour. Guys, we gotta get going. Nice to make your acquaintance."

"Yours too, Tank."

Vinny came over and bear hugged Essie and me. "A guy named Tony will pick the car up here tomorrow if that's okay. And don't forget, if you need anything… Keep my number. You can always get me on that number. And good luck to you finding a new boat. See you around."

We watched as they boarded the sleek black jet and took off. In just seconds they were out of sight. Essie put her arm around my waist as we walked back to the car.

"What a character that Vinny is."

"You think he's really in the mob?"

"Weren't you listening? There is no such thing as the mob."

We took a room at a local hotel overlooking the river. Within a minute of hitting the sheets we were both dead to the world.

3

We woke up late as the days were growing shorter and the sun didn't creep through the blinds until after seven a.m. Even inside, we could look out and tell it was much colder than it had been in Florida. The trees in front of the hotel were barren of leaves and folks getting in their cars had on jackets.

"Well, Essie, we're right back where we started. Once again, my dream is pushed back. Seems like that's been the pattern of my life for many years."

"Cappy, the last month has been so great that I'd be willing to start it all over again this morning. I don't regret any of it. Besides, if you hadn't had some of these problems, we wouldn't have met and then where would we both be?"

"That's true, beautiful. I guess it's just too easy to overlook what's going well and focus on what's not going right. You're always so positive. That's one of the things I love about you."

"Well, the 'L' word, finally."

"I haven't told you how much I love you?"

"You've shown me in a lot of ways, but a woman needs to actually hear the word."

"I'll say it again then. Miss Essie, you are a much-loved woman and I'm the man who loves you. What do you say to that?"

"I'd say it might be good to crawl back under the sheets for a while. I'm suddenly aware that it's too early to get up this morning, if you get my drift."

"I do, Miss Essie."

By the time we got back out of the sack it was now ten a.m. Essie, looking beautiful with a head full of wet auburn hair and still dripping from a hot shower, walked over and gave me a very wet hug.

"So, Cappy; what's on the agenda for today? I think finding a place to stay would be a good idea. We can't live in a hotel room and our floating home is no longer available."

"You're right. I guess that's job one. I also have been thinking that I better go see a lawyer and get some advice on this divorce. Otherwise, everything will be on hold. I know one downtown who I met at the marina. He's young and seems to be an uncorrupted attorney if they make such a creature. I'll call and see if he'll talk with me this morning."

"Sounds great. I'll try to find a cheapo room we can rent somewhere while you do that. Want to meet at Captain Ratty's for lunch?"

"That would be wonderful."

"I'll drop you at the lawyer's office, if he agrees to meet with you, and then I'll take the car over to the airport like Vinny asked us to. I can get a cab back downtown."

"That sounds like a plan to me. Now, how about another kiss?"

* * *

Captain Ratty's was full. I had finished a two-hour session with the attorney and depression was slowly creeping back into my psyche. I ordered a beer at the bar and saved a stool for Essie. I readily admit that as she walked through the door, smiling beautifully, most of the cares of the day disappeared instantly.

God, she was just lovely, inside and out. I waved her over to the bar. With no hint of false modesty, she came over to me, threw her arms around my neck, and gave me a huge kiss. Whatever an old fart like me ever did to deserve someone as young, beautiful and loving as her was beyond me.

"Hey, handsome. How'd things go with the barrister?"

"About like I thought they would. She's got me in a pretty bad vice grip. He says that she can charge me with desertion and ask for everything."

"Now that she's got *Calypso*, she already has everything. What's left to go after?"

"That's the angle that he's taking. He called her attorney and told her, yeah a woman attorney, that I have no money, no job, and only the clothes in my gym bag. He said no judge would expect more."

"That sounds totally reasonable. So what's the problem?"

"He's afraid she'll want me to pay her alimony forever. He's going to tell her that we're going to insist on half of the house, the boat, the furniture and everything we had together if she wants alimony. With the offer that I'll just sign over everything, if she doesn't want a monthly payment, they might just go for that. Since she thinks I'm a bum anyway, the prospect of everything now with no fussing might work. We should know in a week or so he says. What did you do this morning?"

"I went back to the crappy apartments I used to live in and guess what? My old dump is still not rented. We could move in there on a month to month 'til we get things sorted out."

"We may have to if something doesn't happen soon. We don't really have anyplace else to go and, oh yeah, I had to give the lawyer twenty five hundred bucks to handle this. If they settle quickly that's all he'll charge but if it goes to court, I'll have to come up with another five grand. That's about all we have left. Let's spend some of it right now. How about a sandwich and something to drink?"

"That would be marvelous."

We small talked for about a half hour as we ate. We ordered one last beer each. It wasn't like we had any pressing concerns to run off to. It was about that time a couple I recognized from the marina came into Ratty's. They spotted us right off.

"Les. How's it going?"

"Great Dave, Leigh. How about you guys?"

"Come on over and eat with us."

"We just finished, Dave. We've got a beer coming and we could join you for a few minutes."

We grabbed a table near the back. The lunch crowd was thinning out and the room was getting a lot quieter.

They were an interesting couple. With a hundred extra pounds and a Colonel Sander's goatee, Dave looked like Santa Claus and had the happy disposition to go with it. Leigh was a fiery redhead with a great personality. She had been an executive in the corporate world while Dave was a retired Coast Guardsman who had become a local yacht broker. Essie immediately liked them.

"Where's *Calypso*, Les? I heard you were headed south for the winter?"

"We were, Dave. Unfortunately, fate caught up with us in Florida."

I related to them the recent events and how we were back for a while to figure things out. I asked if they knew of any place to rent that might be a little nicer than Essie's old apartment. Neither of us really wanted to go back there. It would seem like a retreat of sorts. I could see that our story was depressing them.

David and Leigh Pfefferkorn

"That's absolutely tragic, guys. I hate that for you. It seemed like everything was going great and then, WHAM, life bites you in the ass again. So you're going to move back into Essie's apartment, eh?"

"We don't want to. We were really enjoying living on the boat. I wish we could find another one and figure out some way to rent it or better yet, keep it up for somebody for the use of it, at least temporarily."

A visual stroke of inspiration washed across Leigh's face. "Dave, what about John Pittman's old boat? He'll never use it again and he's desperate to get rid of it."

"You're right, Leigh. This might be just what Les and Essie are looking for."

"What are you thinking, Dave?"

"There's this old man, maybe eighty-five or so. He has a Gulfstar 43, a 1977 model. Now, she's rough. He hasn't been maintaining it at all for the last ten years. His wife died last year and he says he wants to go home to Minnesota to live out his remaining years. I'm not exaggerating to say the boat is very neglected. It's livable as it is, just not very attractive and I certainly wouldn't go to sea on her 'til I had been through everything on it. He told me to get rid of it and just make the best deal on it I could. I'm sure he'd sell her to you and finance it himself. You could get that boat dirt cheap."

"How cheap is dirt cheap?"

"Less than fifty grand. If you gave him a couple grand up front you'd probably have a payment of four hundred bucks a month. That would be less than renting an apartment."

I looked over at Essie. She was smiling ear to ear.

"When can we see her?"

"How about now? She's in Oriental. We can be there in an hour."

"Let's go."

The boat was named *Peregrine*. Dave and Leigh had not overstated the case for how rough she was. She was tucked into an older marina. Though ragged, her lines were traditional and I was immediately drawn to her.

"What do you think, Essie?"

"You know what I think. I told you; everything always works out like it's supposed to. As much as you loved *Calypso*, this would be a better boat for us once we had her fixed up. It would certainly take a lot of work, some money and time but I'm up to it. We're going to do it. aren't we?"

"If I sign the papers, what's to keep my ex's lawyer from coming after this too?"

"Hell, we'll put it in my name 'til after you're divorced. I'm not married to her; she's got no claims on me. And, if you're good, I mean *really* good to me, I'll give you half of her after your divorce is final."

"Dave, you and Leigh have saved our lives. You have a deal on our end if Mr. Pittman will go along with it."

"Trust me, he will. I'll give him a call right now and you guys can look around on her some more."

"That's great. We'll be onboard. Hey, if he's a 'go' on this, ask him if we can we start staying aboard tonight."

While Dave went to make his call, Essie and I continued to inspect *Peregrine*.

"I don't know if I have the energy to fix her up. I mean, everything on her needs work."

"We'll do it together. We can fix her up enough to live on for now. Some more work and we can day-sail and after that we'll get her seaworthy enough to head south again."

"I know one thing. If we do this, it's certainly going to be the last time. My last dance, you could say."

"That's a great name! Why don't we call her *Last Dance*? I like that. It kind of sums us up as well. You will be my last man and you'll have my last dance."

"I guess you just named her, Essie. *Last Dance* it is. She does have a lot more room than *Calypso*. I love the big aft stateroom and two large heads. Since she's so old, she's narrower than the modern designs. I'll bet she'll go to wind a lot better than the newer hulls."

After twenty minutes of dreaming out loud about how we'd be fixing up the boat, Dave returned. "Here's the deal. Mr. Pittman says for me to just make it happen and he'll go with the deal. So, can you put down twenty five hundred and then three hundred a

month? If you want, and you come into a little money, you pay her
off any time you want."

We looked at each other in dismay. "Captain Dave, you have
just sold a boat. I'll get the cash out of my bag and then can we just
stay aboard?"

"She's all yours. I'll do anything I can to help you get her back
in shape. She's a beautiful old gal. I love these old boats. With a
solid fiberglass hull, I guarantee she's as strong as ever. Just needs
going through."

"You don't have to convince us. We owe you and Leigh more
than you'll ever know."

Leigh came over and gave us both a hug. "How about we go
over to the Oriental Marina tiki bar and celebrate with a cold
one?"

Essie jumped right on the invitation. "We're buying."

By the end of the evening, Essie and Leigh had figured out
where we could get an old car for five hundred bucks. We were
now stable but almost all our cash was gone. Who would have
dreamed twenty-five grand would disappear so fast? Thanks to
Bob Leisey we were still alive and kicking. If I ever saw him
again, I intended to let him know what a powerful impact his
generous gift had made in our lives. After a couple of hours, Leigh
and Dave had to get back to New Bern. They left us on *Last
Dance* for our first night aboard our new ship. We purchased a
bottle of Chardonnay at the marina store and spent the evening
reminiscing about the recent adventures we had been on together.
We were afraid to try to cut on the propane cabin heater until we
had a chance to examine the system, so we spent the night huddled
together under an open sleeping bag left aboard. *Last Dance* felt
like home from the first night.

The next day the extent of the work that was needed on the boat became more obvious. There's the old saying that the two best days on a boat are the day you buy it and the day you sell it. One of those had just passed. However, I was experienced enough to know that if the hull and rig are sound, the rest of the work on a boat is mainly elbow grease. *Last Dance* was made by Gulfstar, a company that had been out of business for almost twenty years. Their boats were production line, sort of the Chevrolets of yachting. They were solid vessels yet also fell victim to some corner cutting during production.

They were famous for leaking ports and this one was no exception. The ports all had water stains under them. Almost the entire interior was made of teak veneer. After a water stain remained on the teak a significant length of time, it would turn the wood a light gray which stood in sharp contrast to the darker unaffected teak. The cabin floor, known as the sole, was badly scarred as well and the cloth ceiling was mildewed everywhere.

I checked the electrical system and to my surprise, everything worked, most notably the fresh water pump. We filled the water tank up and were delighted that the pump would hold pressure to the system. Before long, Essie was up to her ears in Clorox and soap, scrubbing every inch of the interior. I went topside, hooked up a garden hose, and got the same process going on the cockpit and deck. We made a list of the bare necessities for living aboard and maintaining the boat.

Leigh showed up about three in the afternoon with the five hundred dollar car, an old Nissan Sentra with one hundred fifty thousand miles on it. It was old but not to the point of too embarrassing to drive to the store. She came aboard and checked out our work.

"Oh, Essie, this already looks two hundred percent better. And it's starting to smell clean. I hate the smell of a dirty boat. This is a great layout. I like this better than some of the new boats I've seen. You keep this up and she'll be bristol in short order. Hey, we need to have a combination Welcome Back and New Boat party! You say the word and I'll throw one together."

"That sounds like fun, but you probably should let us get the boat moved to a marina somewhere and settled in first. Then we'd love it."

"Okay, guys. I'll tell Dave you're looking for a slip somewhere; maybe he'll have a suggestion."

"That would be great. How about some lunch?"

We went to a new marina that had just opened in Oriental, the Oriental Harbor Marina. It had a large open deck covered by tables with big umbrellas for shade. We had wanted to try it out and this seemed like the perfect time. The deck was just about empty as it was way after lunchtime. We grabbed a table with a view of the harbor and any boats coming in from the channel leading out to the Neuse River.

The owner of the deli came over to the table and took our orders. "I'm Wayne. Welcome to our new place. Can I get you something to drink?"

We each ordered drinks and a sandwich. After such a steamy day of cleaning, a cold beer tasted spectacular.

"This is a nice place. I love the view."

"I agree, Essie. Oriental needed an outdoor place to eat and people-watch, one of our favorite pastimes."

The marina was certainly beautiful, but it had more of a yacht club feel to it and we guessed it was probably out of our price range.

Another group came in and took the table beside us.

"How are you folks today?" Les asked.

"Fine, thanks. You here on a boat?"

"Just barely. Bought one yesterday."

"What did you get?"

"A Gulfstar 43. It's old and a little rag tag but we've already started to clean her up. It's going to be a big project. How about you folks? Sailors?"

"Absolutely. I'm Lou Schroder. This is my wife Helen and our son Chris. We live on a forty foot Endeavour."

"Are you here at this marina?"

"Nope, we're over at SeaGate. Are you familiar with SeaGate?"

"I kept a boat there a number of years ago for a short while. I liked it. It's small and out of the way but reasonably priced and safe. What are the slips going for over there now?"

"For your boat, about two hundred a month. That's a lot less than Oriental or New Bern would be."

"You're right. I'll call them in the morning and see if they have any slips open."

"I know they do. We have friends that left for the Bahamas a couple of days ago. It's right next to our boat, *Zephyr*."

"I'd really like to get that spot. I'll call first thing."

Every once in a while you meet a couple that is like a mirror to you and your own spouse. It's like you've always known them. That's how it was with Lou and Helen from day one. We talked and drank for a while and then took them over to look at *Last Dance* with us. Lou appreciated her lines and went over a lot of what he felt she needed. He even offered to help with any of it he could. They stayed onboard until almost ten p.m. Leigh stayed late as well and had as many Coronas as she felt safe to have and then drive home. We poured a couple of coffees in her and walked the marina docks until we were confident she was good to go.

Lou was extremely knowledgeable about sailboats. He had his five hundred ton open ocean Master's license and had captained everything from ocean going ships to serious blue water yachts. He and Helen had taken their boat all over the Caribbean and the coastal States. Their son Chris was profoundly deaf. He could neither hear nor speak. Helen and Lou both used sign language and Essie quickly learned some key signs so we could include Chris in our conversations. Anything complicated that was said, Helen would sign to Chris for us. He was a fine young man and had served as crew on board whenever he was not away at school. He had a deaf girlfriend and the two were getting ready to move to New York state to attend the Rochester Institute for the Deaf. Chris was to their designated driver for the evening so we burned the midnight oil talking boats, cruising, country music, and life in general.

By noon the next day, I'd made arrangements for a slip in SeaGate Marina. Having kept a previous boat there, I was looking forward to renewing some old friendships. It was only a two-hour trip by boat from Oriental to SeaGate. However, when an untested boat hasn't been moved from a dock in four years, doing anything with it is challenging and not without some degree of risk. Lou and Helen offered to make the trip with us and we readily accepted their offer. In preparation for the trip, I replaced all the fuel filters and changed the engine oil. The engine was a Perkins 4-108, noted for its leaky reliability. There's an old adage about the Perkins: If it don't leak oil, call the manufacturer 'cause it's defective. I felt comfortable that it was running smoothly. If there was a problem with the sails or rigging, we could always motor to SeaGate. I have to say, though, I wanted to see how the old girl sailed.

Last Dance **stretches her legs**

We shoved off from Oriental around nine in the morning. There was a light breeze and the temperature was a perfect sixty-two degrees. We motored out into the Neuse and with a lot of anticipation, I unfurled the mainsail. The mainsail had 'in mast' furling. That meant the sail literally rolled up inside a vertical slot inside the mast. Though I never had this arrangement before, it became obvious immediately that there were problems associated with it. The sail was very tight in the slot and difficult to unfurl. I had to use a winch to get the sail out. Once it was out and the boat started to move with the wind, things began to feel better.

"Essie, kill the engine. Let's see what she'll do."

"Aye, aye, captain. Let's put out the genny."

I began to unfurl the genoa, or headsail. We were now under full sail. *Last Dance* was moving on her own with no help from the motor.

"Not bad. I'm sure the bottom has a nice coating of barnacles. With a clean bottom, I think she'll move along really well. As narrow as she is, I thought she'd sail well."

Essie came up beside me at the wheel. "We're back in business, Cappy."

"Lou, how about you take the wheel for a while so Essie and I can walk around the deck?"

"Absolutely, Cappy. She sure does sail well. These older designs had a lot going for them."

To describe *Last Dance*, I'd have to start with the profile. She's not all that high in the water. That means she has a moderate freeboard for a center cockpit boat. She's a sloop rig with a tiny mainsail and large headsail. I think that came about from wanting a main that could furl into the mast; the smaller the better. She is a headsail driven boat by design. Her cabin trunk has almost vertical sidewalls and there's a good amount of side deck to get around on. She has a small bowsprit that's used to hold the anchors and attach the bow pulpit. Most of her rigging was original and it was apparent some of it could use upgrading as time and money permitted. Money was going to be a real problem when it came to refurbishing the boat. We'd have to make do with what was there as much as possible. The sails were old but serviceable. They had probably been replaced at some point. Down below, *Last Dance* had six foot six inch headroom throughout, with the exception of the walkthrough from the main salon to the aft cabin, which was about five and a half foot due to the cockpit being overhead. There was a large aft master cabin with a queen size bed and a full head with shower. The main salon had a rather small galley with a propane oven and ice box. Refrigeration would need to be added as soon as possible. The salon had settees on port and on starboard that would pull out to make a full size berth on both sides. There was a forward head with a shower and it could be sealed off from the main salon with access only from the forward stateroom when guests were aboard. The V-berth in the forward cabin was large and airy. Most of the interior below was teak and a little on the dark side. With as many water stains as had been caused by port leaks, a lot of the veneer needed replacing. I could fix the leaks quickly with silicone but the veneer would have to wait until we had the money. There was a large engine room that sat amidships. It offered a lot of room to work on the systems that I was certain would need a serious going over and updating. Essie and I both loved the traditional look and feel. I was already developing a plan of attack to bring her back to bristol condition.

After an hour of sitting on the aft deck and watching *Last Dance* sail, we joined Lou and Helen in the cockpit. "Wow, I'm pleased with her. Let me spell you on the wheel, Lou. I appreciate your taking her for so long."

"My pleasure. Sailing has never been work for me. I'd love to help you with some of the projects I know must be running through your head right now. I've had *Zephyr* for over twenty years. She's a similar boat to this and I could give you a lot of tips and contribute some elbow grease."

"You don't know how much I'd appreciate that, Lou."

For the next hour, we sailed slowly toward *Last Dance*'s new home. Helen and Essie got to know each other a lot better.

"I've cruised with Lou for years. I can tell you how to store food so it will last and take up less space. There's one thing I always do before an offshore trip. I make up a large amount of a dinner entrée, such as spaghetti. Then I break it up into individual servings and put them in freezer bags and I freeze them. When we get hungry underway, Lou starts the generator for a short while; I throw the meals in the microwave and we have a hot meal. I've found that's the best way to eat well underway. When Chris is traveling with us, he's always fishing off the stern. If he catches a nice fish, Lou will fillet it and we'll have fresh fish for dinner."

Lou and Helen Schroder

Lou explained how he and Helen got where they were today. "I started out on a small farm in South Dakota. My dad was dairy farmer. It was a shoestring operation. I had to get up at four in the morning, even while I was in school, and milk the cows. Of course, they'd be waiting for me again when I got home from school. I got used to working hard early on. Right out of school I joined the Air Force and got trained as an electrician. When I got out, I worked as a repair technician in the printing press business. They sent me all over the world repairing them. I learned to fly and eventually became a corporate pilot, still traveling. I guess when you're raised on a remote farm in an isolated corner of the world, you want to see as many other places as you can.

"I eventually got into the machine shop business in Pennsylvania. I was married with two girls and making a lot of money. I bought a small sailboat and started thinking about going cruising. Eventually I sold the business and my marriage started falling apart. I had met Helen twenty years prior through her brother, Hollis, that I worked with. Just about the same time I was going through my divorce, she wound up doing the same thing. We got together like we should have been all along. Meanwhile, I'd bought *Zephyr* and got my Captain's License. When our

divorces were final, we got married and we've been sailing together ever since then."

Helen was born in Kansas, a farm girl, and she loved to joke that she had ridden the Chisholm Trail. Being completely naïve and uninformed about western lore, I fell for it, hook, line and sinker. Chris was not Helen's birth child. He was the child of her brother and was not getting the sort of home life she knew he deserved. After he became sick and lost his hearing and voice as an infant, Helen offered to adopt him and her brother agreed. Helen had been a special education teacher for her entire career and was ideally suited to care for a child such as Chris. She raised him as her own and he never knew his history until she felt he was old enough to understand. Today, Helen, Lou, and Chris are family. They all love cruising and living aboard. Lou now took occasional jobs as a Captain for the fun and experience. He was certainly a wealth of information about the seas and sailing. I determined I'd pick his brain all I could.

"Les, here's our turn into the marina. I'll get your bow lines."

"Great. Essie would you get the stern?"

"Done."

Helen joined in. "How about I stay in the cockpit here to witness the crash?"

Lou looked at her and smiled. "Ignore her, Les. She's a smartass from time to time."

All in all it had been a good day. *Last Dance* had no real problems on the move. We had gotten to know Lou and Helen a lot better. They were a couple that we instantly felt we had a lot in common with, other than they had done and were doing what we hoped to do one day soon. We spent another great evening in the cockpit until the cold caught up with us and we said goodnight. It was now December and though the days got up to the low sixties most of the time, the nights were getting pretty darn cold. We bought a small electric heater and a heavy comforter. Essie and I quickly made the aft cabin our personal castle. We would put a soft CD on and curl up.

"Cappy, we sure got a stroke of luck on *Last Dance*, didn't we?"

"I'd say so. It would be pretty embarrassing though to have to tell Long John that the one thing he gave us money for is the furthest away from what we're doing right now, namely cruising."

"He'd understand. We're doing all we can. We're not in charge of the world. All we can do is live every day the best we can, not waste a moment of the time we're given."

"That's what I love the most about you, Essie. You're my lemonade queen, always making lemonade out of lemons. If it weren't for you, I'd be pretty down right about now."

"Down? Why down? You're with a loving woman on a great boat that you practically stole and soon, probably this spring, we'll be heading back to paradise on her."

"I hope you're right. There is still the matter of work though."

"Work?"

"Yep. I've got to find a job to make money to not only replenish what I've had to spend but to hopefully fix up the boat and refill the cruising kitty. We can live pretty darn cheap onboard but I've got to make some money."

"What are you thinking about doing? The closest place to work is New Bern. What could you do there?"

"Not much. Maybe mow lawns."

"You're not really thinking about doing that, are you?"

"It's certainly not above me, but I'm afraid I need to make a little more money than that would pay."

"I don't want you to do something you hate. That makes every day miserable and affects everything else about your life. What would you like to do if you could do anything you want?"

"I'd probably enjoy writing."

"Like a book?"

"Exactly, and maybe some magazine articles to help make a few bucks in between."

"Is that possible to do? I always heard it was almost impossible to get a book published."

"Same here. But I think I'll start heading in that direction. You know, there's something else ridiculous I think I could do."

"And that would be?"

"I think I could get a job playing guitar and singing at the local bars and restaurants around here. There sure are a lot of them and they're all trying to outdo each other."

"Do you have a guitar?"

"I guess my ex has probably burned it already. But I can get one pretty cheap at a pawn shop. What do you think?"

"I've always thought you had a great voice but I never thought about you singing for your supper, so to speak."

"I once heard that you should never be upset about singing for your supper because the guy on the other end of the spoon is working for a song."

"That's cute, very insightful."

"If you don't think it's a stupid idea, I'm going to try and get a gig doing just that. I'll check around tomorrow for a guitar and see if can I get an evening job. Would you play the tambourine and sing harmony with me?"

"I'd probably be terrified to sing in front of people, but after a couple of Cosmos, who knows? Maybe I'm a Loretta Lynn in the rough. I'll make you a deal."

"And that would be?"

"I'll sing with you at whatever place you can find that's desperate enough to hire us and you'll stop all the negative talk, start writing a book, and get *Last Dance* ready to go by March."

"Is that all you want?"

"You want a high-dollar woman, you have to be willing to pay the price. Put up or shut up."

"Okay, you've got a deal. However, I'm chilly and I think a high-dollar woman might be just the ticket right about now."

"Oh, you're an instant gratification type of guy, I see."

"Not instantly, but slowly, gently over the next hour or so would be good."

4

Life was good on board *Last Dance*. Most of the next month was spent making her livable and presentable. There were hundreds of details to check which usually resulted in a repair or upgrade. Problems with systems on a sailboat are far less a problem when they're discovered and fixed at the dock. Everything can't be foreseen but offshore in a blow is not the time to be repairing things. I had tried out for a number of jobs playing guitar in area restaurants, but most places felt it was too close to winter to be investing money in entertainment for a seasonal business. We were just about broke. As if that weren't enough to deal with, my attorney had set up an appointment to try and negotiate a settlement with my ex-wife and her attorney. I knew that wouldn't be pleasant, but since I didn't have the thousands needed to go to court, I pretty much had to strike the best bargain I could at the meeting. Essie drove me to Raleigh for the meeting.

"Good luck, Cappy. I'll entertain myself at the mall for few hours. Give me a call when you're ready for me to pick you up."

"God, I hope this doesn't go as badly as everything else related to this mess has so far."

"It will work out the way it's supposed to. Stay positive."

"I'll try."

Essie passed the time away at the bookstore, thumbing through sailing and travel magazines. Her thoughts weren't generally far away from mine. We both wanted to find a way to a simpler, more rewarding life, one with a lot less of the complications presented to the average family. When my meeting was over, I called her to come pick me up.

"Hey, sweetness. How did it go? Will you be reporting to the county jail anytime soon?"

"It actually went better than I thought it would."

"How's that?"

Her attorney was smart enough to know I don't have any income and my prospects aren't very good. I made it real clear to them I'd leave the country if they even thought about trying to get alimony from me. My ex has her teaching certificate and a job. She can work just like I can. They demanded, and I agreed to sign over everything I own except the clothes on my back. They already have somebody interested in *Calypso* so they want all the money from that sale. She'll get what retirement I have coming from my old job and everything in the house. The kids are all over twenty-one so there's no issue of child support. I was pretty much in a corner so I agreed. I don't own anything now, after forty some years of busting my ass, but at least I'm shed of her."

"Good grief. What a selfish bitch! But I wouldn't say you don't have anything. You have me, and as soon as your paperwork is all done on the divorce, we'll draw up the documentation papers on *Last Dance* and you'll be a partner with me in owning her. What else do you need?"

"How 'bout a beer? I think I need one of those."

"Let's head back to New Bern. In two hours we can be back at Captain Ratty's for a late lunch and then I'll treat you to a couple of beers. Besides, I'd like to see Tom. If it weren't for Captain Ratty's we wouldn't be here together today."

"Lead on."

We arrived at Ratty's just as the lunch crowd was thinning out. We each got a stool at the bar, ordered a beer and a sandwich. After fifteen or so minutes, Tom showed up.

"Les, Essie, what in blue blazes are you doing here? I thought you'd be in the Bahamas or Dry Tortugas about now."

"In a nutshell, my previous life caught up with us in Florida. We were just getting going when the local constable served me with divorce papers and put an injunction on my boat. We've been back just about a month. We've already found a new boat, and settled the divorce today. We came to celebrate with you."

"You're heading back south immediately?"

"Can't. We're broke. Between the lawyer and the boat we've broken the bank. We've got to find a job and replenish the kitty."

"What are you looking to do?"

"To be honest, I had the ridiculous thought that I might play guitar and sing at some bars. Called on a few and can't find any takers."

"Well, my friend, you just found one."

"Seriously?"

"Absolutely. As long as you're cheap. Say a hundred bucks a night plus whatever customers throw in your tip jar. Of course, that's all dependent on you not being terrible."

"I haven't played for money for thirty years or so, but I still pick up the guitar from time to time."

Essie offered a reference. "He's fabulous, Tom. You won't be sorry. When can we start?"

"We? You play too?"

"I'm going to be his tamboriness."

"What the heck is a tamboriness?"

"That's short for beautiful female assistant who plays the tambourine."

"I should have known that. What was I thinking?"

"Tell you what, 'til further notice, we'll try Thursday through Sunday evenings. Will that work for you?"

"I'll start working on my song list immediately. All right, Tom. A Corona for me and a Cosmo for the tamboriness."

"Coming up. Now, tell me all about your trip. *Calypso*'s on the auction block, eh?"

"They said today they think she's sold. I wish the new owner well. He helped me buy my way out of the divorce. It's just me and Essie now and our new boat *Last Dance*."

"Tell me all about it."

* * *

Thursday came quickly. I hadn't had nearly the time to practice I wanted. We told a lot of our sailing friends about what we were doing and Ratty's upstairs bar was packed. Lou and Helen had front row seats. This was a little nerve racking but not nearly as bad as working at the Bible factory under Dalton Smythewicke. Nothing could be as bad as that. I felt I needed to start with a song I knew I could play in my sleep. That would have to be Roger Miller's classic "King of the Road." It was an up tempo song and my friends were helping out by singing along on the chorus. Essie was kicking butt on the tambourine and before long the place was jumping. Tom beamed from ear to ear at the boisterous crowd that would not normally be there on a Thursday evening in winter.

The first hour went by almost instantly it seemed. We took a break and visited with the friends who had gone out of their way to offer support. My good friend Larry Basden came by. He brought with him his main squeeze, Linda Jo. She was an outgoing redhead, and she helped out with harmony the rest of the evening. No one seemed surprised that I was getting a divorce. I guess that by the time we're old enough and smart enough to make the right decisions, we've already made most of our life's decisions, and apparently a lot of them weren't too good. More than one friend suggested that my next missus was playing the tambourine that evening.

By the end of the second set, the group had polished off a truckload of beer. They were singing along with every song. After all, the songs I knew were all from the sixties and seventies. That was the time period all of us were from, when songs actually had stories to them and you could understand the words. The party was upstairs in Captain Ratty's piano bar. The building was over a hundred years old with wide planked wooden floors and exposed brick walls. The sound reverberated from the ceiling beams and with everyone in the room accompanying me on each song, it must have sounded like Woodstock to anyone walking down the street in front of the building. As we started to wrap the evening up, I was down to repeating some of the same songs as I had exhausted my repertoire and realized I needed to work on that if I was going to continue to do this.

Essie had a ball and loved the attention. "Cappy, this was fun. I could see us making a living doing this while we cruise. I knew you could play and sing, but I really didn't know you were this good. Where did you learn to play?"

"I had a band in high school. Several of the guys went on to become professional musicians. But that's a long story. And we've got a long ride home. I'll tell you on the way. Lou and Helen are driving, aren't they?"

"We came with them. I can't see them making us thumb back to the boat."

"Great. We can sit in the back seat and neck. Just like high school. Or at least like I wished it would have been in high school. To say the least, I was not a hot commodity in my teens. Actually, I've never been considered much of a catch. I think women looked at me as the marrying kind, not the mess around and have fun with kind."

Essie gave me the prettiest smile I'd ever seen and kissed me squarely on the lips. "This was a nostalgia trip evening for you, wasn't it?"

"My songs, my people. What can I say? My generation invented rock and roll."

There were three more evenings to play that first weekend but the first night's success had me believing that Essie was right and we would be able to get on with our lives again, especially the cruising part. On the way home amidst all the talk about music and the times we grew up in, it was decided that we would take *Last Dance* and follow Lou and Helen on *Zephyr* for our first cruise on the new boat. We'd go to Cape Lookout on Monday morning since we wouldn't have to be back at Ratty's until the following Thursday. Essie was right as usual. Things were looking better.

The first weekend at Ratty's had been very encouraging. By Saturday night we were drawing some folks we didn't know. Some were tourists and others had heard we were pretty good from some of those who were there earlier in the week. I felt like we were going to be able to survive. I couldn't wait until Monday came so we could take *Last Dance* out for her shakedown cruise.

We got off to a late start so I could get in the water and clean the bottom with a scraper. There were a lot of barnacles so I knew that I'd be doing this nasty job until I could pull her and repaint the bottom with antifouling. I borrowed a wet suit from Lou but even then it was pretty dang cold. I did get most of the barnacles off and even cleaned the prop. Lou and Helen left earlier and agreed to meet us in the bight at Cape Lookout. They wanted to sail a little out in the ocean while they waited for us.

By noon we were headed south on Adam's Creek. It was a warm afternoon for January. Cape Lookout would be practically deserted this time of year, especially mid-week. There was very little traffic on Adam's creek. It's a narrow body of water that connects the Neuse River to the Newport River and Beaufort. The middle section is a man-made canal. The VHF radio was on and turned up loud so we could hear any approaching barge traffic. It's good to know if you're going to be sharing the channel with any commercial vessels as it's a narrow passage.

Essie and I delighted in how well the old boat motored and the ease with which she cut through the water. She was large and heavy. The feeling that she was an extremely seaworthy vessel took hold of us. We contacted *Zephyr* on the radio to see how their day was going.

"Lou, you guys having a good time?"

"Couldn't be better. Great wind. Plenty of sun. Where are you guys?"

"We're just clearing Adam's Creek. Probably too late to make Lookout tonight. How 'bout meeting us in Beaufort? We can both get a slip at the town docks and grab dinner together."

"Sounds good. We'll see you there."

We continued motoring across the Newport River, up Gallant's Channel and turned into Taylor Creek. We immediately noticed the large black schooner that was at the T-dock on the end of the second pier. As we approached we could see the beautiful vessel was an exact replica of the *America*. Back in the 19th century, the original schooner *America* that the America's Cup was named for sailed to England and defeated all of Britain's fastest vessels of that day.

Shortly we would learn that this replica was made from the same blueprints as the original and was beautiful. She was a charter boat and was moving south toward Key West where she would take paying guests on two-hour sails during the day and champagne sundown cruises every evening. This day she was open so paying guests could tour her. There appeared to be dozens on board checking her out. We motored past her and then turned into the four knot current of Taylor Creek where we were instructed by the Beaufort town dock master to tie up to the T dock on the next pier down from her. As we passed slowly by, we marveled that such a spectacular vessel was based on such an old design. Her lines were still magnificent.

"After we get settled, let's see if Lou and Helen want to tour the *America*."

"You got it, Cappy. What can I do to help us tie up?"

"How about going up to the bow and tie a dock line to the center cleat. Be prepared to drop it over a cleat on the dock. You'll be pretty high over the dock since they're floating. There doesn't seem to be anyone on the dock to take the line so just loop it over the dock cleat and secure both ends on the bow cleat."

"Aye, aye, skipper."

I eased *Last Dance* slowly toward the dock directly in front of the *America*. The wind was over twenty knots and blowing directly toward the shore and the finger pier. I proceeded forward as slowly as I could make headway. Essie stood on the foredeck, dock line in hand. All seemed in order. I slowed to a complete stop directly centered off the finger pier, with less than a foot between the hull and the pier.

Just as we got ready to touch the dock, a small wake from a passing power boat kissed the side of the boat and as I looked forward, Essie lost her balance and did a complete summersault off the bow right toward the floating wooden dock about six feet below. I couldn't see whether she struck the dock or the water from my viewpoint. She didn't call out or scream and I heard no splash. *Last Dance* was still in forward, idling to keep the current from taking us quickly into the bow of the *America*, less than twenty-five feet directly behind us. Taylor Creek has a swift current and the water is deep. I knew if Essie had struck her head on the dock and was unconscious, she would be gone in seconds. My first thought was to shut off the prop in case she drifted with the current under the boat where it would cut her to shreds. I threw the boat into neutral. It wasn't tied to the dock yet and I knew in less than a minute it would slam into the *America*.

I determined I would count to five and if I didn't see her, I would dive overboard and whatever happened to the boats would just have to happen. Saving Essie was really all that mattered at that moment. The seconds seemed to last an hour as I counted each one out. Just as I reached four, I saw a silver haired man running toward us on the dock. He reached out his hand and in only two seconds I saw a drenched Essie being dragged from the water onto the pier with him. Undoubtedly, he had saved her life.

Filled immediately with an overriding sense of relief, I ran forward and tossed a line to the man who secured *Last Dance* to the finger pier. He had saved not only Essie but God only knows how much damage a collision between us and the *America* would have caused. I don't like to even think about it. I've joked with Essie many times since this event about what a phone call between me and my insurance company would have sounded like.

"Hello, this is the Claims Department. May I help you?

"You certainly may. This is Les Pendleton and my boat is insured with you."

"Yes, sir. What can I do for you today?"

"I've got some good news and some bad news."

"Go ahead, sir."

"Thanks, the good news is that my boat has been holed and is a total loss."

"That's the good news?"

"Yes, and the bad news is we sank the schooner *America* with fifty tourists on board. I think you're going to get out of this all for somewhere around fifty million!"

Silence.

Obviously, that would not be funny and thank God I didn't have to make that call. The silver-haired gentleman who had saved Essie and tied up *Last Dance* came over to the cockpit where I was cutting off the motor. "Sir, I can't possibly thank you enough. My name is Les Pendleton."

"No problem, skipper. I'm Stuart Stovall. My wife Shelia is just now coming down the dock. Are you folks okay?"

"We are now thanks to you, Stuart.

Essie came over to me with a dazed look on her face and thanked him herself. She quickly regained her composure after assuring us she was no worse for wear. "I just want to get on some dry clothes and get a glass of wine. Why don't you invite these folks to have dinner with us, Cappy? On us, of course."

We certainly didn't have the money to buy dinner for anyone else, barely for ourselves, but there was no mistaking that this was the least we could do in this situation. "Stuart, would you and Shelia care to join us for a bite at Clawson's? There's another couple joining us as well that I'm sure you'll enjoy meeting."

"That sounds fine with us. We were just going to tour the *America* and then eat ourselves."

"Well, after our friends pull in, we'll join you for the tour as well."

Stuart and Shelia Stovall

By the time Essie had dried her hair and put on some clean clothes, Lou and Helen had pulled *Zephyr* in alongside us. I gave them a brief account of what had just happened and explained our new plans. They still wanted to come along.

We met the Stovalls at the gangplank leading up to *America*. The crowd had thinned considerably. As we walked about on her deck, one of the hands on board her yelled out, "Look, it's the lady that did the swan dive off the sailboat in front of us." Initially Essie was a little embarrassed, but after a little back and forth banter with the crew, she enjoyed the fact that she had now met the crew of the fabled schooner.

Two years later, we were in Key West and noticed that the *America* was tied up in front of Schooner's Wharf Bar. We walked over to inquire the rate for the sunset cruise and the guy selling tickets immediately yelled out to the other crewmembers, "Look, it's the lady who did the swan dive off her boat in Beaufort!" Essie took it all good-naturedly and we all reminisced for a while. They were a little upset with us when we took the evening cruise on the *Western Union* instead, as it was almost half the price.

Lou and Helen, Miss Essie and I, and the Stovalls finished up the boat tour and had a lovely dinner and drinks at Clawson's, a well-known Beaufort watering hole that is probably the best food in Beaufort short of the Royal James. Lou loved the Royal James more than any restaurant on the planet. I will admit they make some of the best old fashioned, greasy cheeseburgers on the planet. Other than the food, it's mostly a pool hall and bar just a short walk from the waterfront. It wasn't on our schedule this evening however.

We left Clawson's and headed for another Beaufort landmark, the Backstreet Pub. This little hole-in-the-wall is a two-story rock and roll joint set up in an old home on the street just behind Front Street. It's a rowdy place with a patron mix of sailors, young people, and old Dead Header's who can't get enough of sixties rock and roll. This evening there was a band playing that looked to be about sixty years old on average. Some of them looked as though they needed a walker to get on stage. However, when they started to play it was apparent they had cut their teeth on this music and they still felt it. Quite appropriately, their name was *The Relics*. Quickly, we were all moving to the music. The songs were great, the beer was cold, and all three couples were having an absolute ball. After we had all had a few adult beverages, the ladies decided they needed to visit the restroom. It was located upstairs and required elbowing their way through a shoulder-to-shoulder crowd. There was a line to use the facility and they all felt they might pop before their turn. When Essie became next in line she said to the other ladies, "Look, let's all just go in together. It'll be quicker for us all that way."

However, Essie was not aware just how small the bathroom was. There was only one small toilet and a sink sitting on top of a miniature cabinet with a mirror above it. They had waited long enough so Essie did her business and scooted away from the toilet still pulling up her blue jeans.

It was about this time that Helen exclaimed. "Good Lord, Essie. You have a bruise on your leg the size of a basketball! That looks terrible."

"Oh my God! Where?"

"Just below your cheek on the right side. You must have done it when you fell off the boat."

"Well, I fell so hard I literally broke the stainless life line in front of me. Here, let me step up on the vanity and see it in the mirror." Essie put one foot on the rim of the toilet, hiked her other foot onto the edge of the sink and backed up to the mirror. She was bent over with her pants down around one ankle checking out her backside in the mirror while Helen and Shelia looked on.

Just then the unlocked door opened and a young woman entered totally oblivious to the fact the room was already occupied. She first looked at Helen and Shelia and then noticed they were staring at this other woman's butt while she was straddling the sink and the toilet. The girls all looked over to the intruder and just smiled. What was there to say? God only knows what she thought was going on in there but without saying a word, she backed out of the room and shut the door behind her. Simultaneously, Essie, Helen and Shelia broke out in a belly laugh. It's a story they would still be re-telling many years later.

We became instant friends with Stuart and Shelia that evening, as did Lou and Helen. We all agreed over the last pitcher of draft beer and the ladies' Cosmos that Stuart and Shelia would come with us in the morning aboard *Last Dance* as we completed the trip to Cape Lookout.

Tuesday's dawn broke beautifully over Beaufort. Stuart and Shelia had stayed aboard with us. We all went aboard *Zephyr* for a breakfast of bacon and eggs, country sausage, and my own contribution, my world famous lighter-than-helium pancakes. The only thing in the world I can cook is these pancakes so I take great pride in them. I've been told many times that the Pancake House restaurants can't touch 'em. I agree. We all ate too much but knew we needed to get underway.

Stuart and Shelia had never sailed on a large sailboat so they were looking forward to the experience tremendously. As a young boy, Stuart had a small day sailer but had not spent any time since then on a sailboat. To say he was eager would be understatement. The wind was perfect and we were able to hold a very steady broad reach all the way to Cape Lookout. That trip covers about six miles of ocean sailing each way in the Atlantic. There was a gentle swell running and *Last Dance* gracefully climbed and descended each wave effortlessly. I should have been suspicious there was something going on during that sail with Stuart. He held the wheel the entire trip and seemed to be in a zone of deep concentration for the full two hours. Essie, Shelia and I listened to music and chatted during that time as we got to know their story.

The Stovalls were from the small town of Angier located about a forty-minute drive south and east of Raleigh. Stuart was in the telephone business among other things. He was considering selling out and searching for something to fill his days. Little did we know we helped him find what that something would be that very day: Stuart found out he loved sailing and sailboats.

Within a week of returning from this trip to Cape Lookout, he bought a 31' sloop to be replaced less than four months later by a 43' Irwin. Shortly after buying the Irwin, Stuart informed me that he had sold his business and was going to cruise indefinitely. He then said he had enrolled in The Landing School in Maine where he would become ABYC licensed in marine systems. The Landing School is very prestigious and the only place in the United States that offers this certification, which is used to determine "best practices" for building and repairing all types of yachts virtually worldwide.

Stuart completed the school in a year and then proceeded to take Shelia on what he called a cruise of no predetermined length where they would go until they had it out of their system. Within a year Stuart called and said he was coming back to trade boats, which he did. Today, they are in South Africa sailing around the world on their Stephens Custom Offshore 47. He has told me numerous times since we met that I had dramatically changed their lives. I hope in the end I'll be getting "credit" and not "blame." In all honestly, I wanted to go with them so badly I can't describe it. But I had no business to sell and thus was grounded by poverty to a life of wishing once again.

However, today the ocean was spectacular. There was a gentle two-foot swell so that *Last Dance* rose gently up one side and slowly down the other. The motion would easily put you to sleep. Stuart steered us toward Cape Lookout as we loaded a song on the CD player and relaxed. Essie lay on the cockpit seat with her feet in my lap. As she nodded off I took in the beauty of the translucent blue ocean around me. If you could pick a time and place to spend eternity, this would be it for me. Around four p.m. we turned toward the Cape Lookout bight. We had stalled as long as we could.

"We better head in Essie. Lou and Helen will be waiting on us to grill some steaks, I'm sure. I guess we'll just raft up with them for dinner. If it stays this calm we could both lay off on his anchor for the night. If it picks up a little, we break free and set our own anchor."

"I was sleeping like a baby. What a marvelous afternoon. I guess I better quit dreaming and wake up."

"What kind of dreams where you having?"

"Well, we were both in them."

"Is that right? What were we doing?"

"All I'm going to say is that we were both dressed a lot better than we are now and a lot of our friends were there."

"I can think of only one situation where that might occur."

"I'm not saying another word. How far to the bight?"

"About thirty minutes."

Cape Lookout has been described as The Poor Man's Bahamas. It's easy to see where this comparison comes from. On this part of the coast where the rivers are dark and muddy, the bight is unusually pristine with fairly clear water averaging around twenty-five feet in depth. It's washed clean by the ocean every twelve hours as the tide changes. The turtle lovers come here in the spring to help the loggerheads survive hatching. On some trips I've seen hundreds of loggerheads swimming in the bight. At first glance, they always startle watchers as they appear to be someone swimming or floating in the water. Their heads are about the same size as a person's and they float just below the surface with only their heads showing. On holiday weekends, the bight is packed with boats of all types. The Cape Lookout lighthouse sits on the ocean side of the barrier island that creates the bight. The outer bank here is crescent shaped and is only a small line of dunes that separates the calm water in the bight from the ocean. The light from the lighthouse reflects across the entire harbor throughout the night. I've sat many evenings entranced by its beacon and watched as it danced off the waves and the boats anchored there. There are no homes of any type on the banks as it's a national seashore, just a museum and a ranger compound. The beaches are pristine and, with the exception of all the yachts there, it must look pretty much the same as it has for the past three hundred years. It's about four miles to the site of the sunken *Queen Anne's Revenge*. She was the flagship of the notorious pirate Blackbeard. He is believed to have scuttled the ship himself shortly before his death at the hands of troops in Ocracoke forty some miles farther north.

We approached *Zephyr* slowly. Lou had his fenders out and lines handy to help us tie up alongside. "Howdy folks. Nice day wasn't it?"

"Beautiful Lou, and I believe we've got Stuart hooked."

"I figured that was going to happen with a day like this one."

Needless to say, by the time we arrived at Cape Lookout, Stuart was in fact bitten hard by the sailing bug and wanted to talk with Lou and me about boats the remainder of the trip. The girls bonded like sisters who had been separated at birth. The two rafted boats bobbed gently to the movement of the water in the protected bight where we were anchored. The sun was beautiful while it lasted but by early evening it started to descend as did the thermometer. We moved below in *Zephyr* where several bottles of wine were opened and the stereo was loaded with soft jazz and country CDs. We talked about so many things that evening that it's hard to remember just one story. But I do know that friendships were initiated that weekend that will carry on until we are all dust.

Lou and Helen were the epitome of kindred spirits for Essie and me. Lou was knowledgeable, helpful, and had a bit of a cantankerous side to him, especially if your politics and his were different. He came from the old school. He had worked hard, had been given nothing, had made his fortune and retired in his early forties. Helen was as sweet and endearing as Lou was contrary. She was the buffer he needed. Theirs was a solid relationship based on genuine respect and affection for each other. As long as they had known each other; even before they married, they knew what they were getting into. Together, they had sailed *Zephyr* for countless miles, seen things and experienced so much of the sailing that I was still yearning to do. I could listen to their stories for hours on end. After a great evening of such tales, a couple bottles of wine and a slightly increasing wind, we decided to separate the two boats. If the wind were to pick up any more, two vessels of the size of our boats might start to drag anchor. I certainly didn't want to be awakened at three in the morning as *Last Dance*'s keel started to touch bottom. We found a nice spot about fifty yards away from Lou and dropped the hook. We were in about twenty feet of water with a great view of the lighthouse. Essie and I stayed up an hour or so after the Stovalls hit the bed, rubbing each other's shoulders and sweet talking. Just before we were about to fall asleep in the cockpit, we realized it was getting cold and went below to our large aft bunk.

Sometime in the middle of the night I awoke with a start. I don't know what sense it is in sailors that will wake them just as a boat begins to drag anchor or some other noteworthy event starts occurring. Nothing was wrong, but I was awake and as always when that happened decided to go topside and take a look around. Maybe we were slipping a little.

Just as I got halfway up the companionway steps, *Last Dance* was struck by something in the water hard enough to make her rock five or six degrees from port to starboard several times. Somewhat startled, I grabbed the handholds on either side of the companionway and moved quickly up into the cockpit. As I looked around I noticed the strangest sight. On top of the otherwise calm water of the bight, there was a large wake in the shape of a V moving away from the center of *Last Dance* and headed directly toward *Zephyr*. I watched awestruck until I saw it literally bump into the side of *Zephyr* causing her to rock in the same manner that we had just experienced. That's a pretty serious motion for a boat that weighs over fifteen tons. Seconds later, I saw Lou in the cockpit. He stepped on the deck and looked toward us. With the moonlight illuminating the harbor, he could plainly see that I was up too and he called over to me.

"What the hell was that?"

"Don't know. Whatever it was, it was big, really big."

To this day, I don't have a clue what was swimming in the bight that night. Whatever it was, I don't understand why it was unable to tell it was running into things. Or maybe the creature meant to disturb us that night. Cape Lookout bight is out in the ocean a pretty good ways so I suppose anything could be in the water. I know that I always think twice before swimming out there. The water is beautiful and inviting but it's also deep and full of nature.

It does bring to mind a similar experience that Essie and I experienced one night in Town Creek at Beaufort. We were on a weekend cruise with a number of other boats. We were anchored in only seven feet of water in a very small, secluded harbor. There was no wind and never any waves in there. It was only a hundred yards from Town Creek Marina. We had had dinner at a local restaurant and then a nightcap on a friend's boat that was berthed in a slip at the marina. Essie and I headed back to *Calypso* in our eight and half foot inflatable dinghy about one a.m. There was no wind and the water looked like a mirror. The dinghy had only a three horsepower motor and we were moving at around four knots toward the swim platform on our stern. As we got to within ten or fifteen feet from the platform of our boat, something rammed our dinghy hard enough to knock it off course by at least thirty degrees. It splashed as it struck us. It was not a casual collision. It was aggressive and sharp. We scrambled up from the dinghy and safely onto *Calypso* as quick as we ever had. We just stared out for several minutes in our newly sober state and watched to see if anything disturbed the water surface again, but there was nothing. Once again, we had no idea what would have done this or why. The water was not clear or very clean and this was right in the middle of a small, congested anchorage. These two events always give me some pause when going overboard in dark water.

Morning came. Essie and I were forced to sleep in and small talk for at least an extra hour so as not to awaken our boat guests with our morning routine. I have always loved breakfast onboard a sailboat. After the Stovalls woke up, we took our dink and motored over to *Zephyr*. The smell of fresh coffee wafting out of the salon greeted us before we even pulled alongside. Lou took our lines and in only a moment we were being served a hot cup of coffee to take the chill out of the winter morning. Helen was hard at work below preparing the fixings of a breakfast masterpiece. She had sweet rolls, fried or scrambled eggs, sausage and bacon, toast and jelly, grits and orange juice. Of all the women I've ever met, I don't think I ever knew one that enjoyed having company to fuss over as much as Helen. Lou had done his best day's work when he married her.

We ate until we felt like overinflated weather balloons. The girls went below to straighten up after the feast and Lou, Stuart, and I remained topside where Lou related to us his first cruise across the ocean from Baltimore to Bermuda. He had run into several gales one day. He actually pushed hard for twenty-four hours and when he took his bearings, he'd lost forty miles. He had a great love and respect for the sea. I envied him for all the years he'd spent sailing while I was working my butt off trying to survive. With Essie, I hoped we could accomplish even ten percent of what Lou and Helen had done on their boat.

By noon, we were all talked out and ready to start the journey back to SeaGate. It seemed that these small cruises took forever to start and then lasted ten minutes. Lou loved country music and said that he and Helen would come to hear Essie and me at Ratty's on Friday night. The Stovalls said they would be there as well. With the number of friends, new and old, that said they were coming that night, I should have seen what was to become forever-known as The Rowdy Ratty's Party.

5

Essie and I arrived early to set up. We had our list of songs built up to around thirty. We could do four hours of music and a little bantering with the audience in between and keep everyone entertained without repeating ourselves. We went downstairs and tried to find a table where we could grab a bite to eat before we had to get to work. Being a Friday, and with a convention at the Riverfront Convention Center, the place was packed. We looked the dining area over and figured we'd just have to take our sandwiches upstairs and eat them on the stools we used when we were making music.

"You folks care to join us?"

I looked over to the back corner where the familiar voice had come from and saw Stuart and Shelia with a pitcher of beer in front of them calling to us. "Cappy, Essie, join us. We've come to try out the entertainment here tonight."

"Well, you guys are asking for it."

We pulled up a couple of chairs and joined them. They were both obviously ready to party.

"It's not like you're here for an Elvis concert. I'm pretty much starting over and, as you can see, I'm not what you'd call a 'headliner' making a big living with my guitar."

We small talked while we ate and after a short while Lou and Helen arrived and joined us. They pulled up two more chairs and we all ordered another pitcher.

"Well folks, it's time for Essie and me to get upstairs and earn our keep."

"We'll go on up with you. Stu, do you and Shelia want to join us and grab a table close to the band?"

"Absolutely. I feel a party coming on."

Our performance started innocently enough. We did a couple of James Taylor songs and watched in amazement as the room filled. Lou's table had become the centerpiece of the room. Other friends arrived and they would pull additional chairs up to the table. Within an hour, not only were the Stovalls and Schroders there, but Dave and Leigh Pfefferkorn too. Larry and Linda Jo came in with Ron and Connie Cousino whom we hadn't seen since Charleston, and then in came friends Paul and Holly Jones. Needless to say, the place was rocking. Dave, who is a talented musician, brought his old Martin guitar and joined us for the last several songs in the first set. We were close enough to the table that we could hear all of their comments and suggestions. They were requesting special favorites one after another. The ones I didn't know, Dave did, and vice-versa. The only thing happening faster than our singing their requested songs was their waitress hauling pitchers of beer, two at a time, to their table. It was in the midst of all this frivolity that a most unexpected customer entered the bar area and moved up toward us.

"Son of a gun, Essie, look who just walked in."

We both said his name together. "It's Grimshaw!"

Jim came up to where we were playing and stood alongside pretending to play the guitar with his best Jimi Hendrix impression. We motioned for Lou to grab him a chair with them, which he handled immediately. Before the song was over, Grimshaw had matriculated with the group of rebel rousers at the 'family' table. I heard him over our music announcing, "Next round's on me. Barkeep, three more pitchers of your finest please."

I could tell from the amount of beer going to the table and the amount of noise leaving the table, this was going to be one hell of an evening. Since Dave was on stage playing with us, Leigh, a fifty plus year old 'wild child' was left unchaperoned at the table with Grimshaw. As we started playing "Margaritaville," they took to the floor with what could best be described as a variation of the Charleston coupled with the Samba. They were a blur of spinning and gyrating that ended with Leigh on top of the table, barefooted with the rest of our group of miscreants clapping and encouraging her to give it her all. And she did. When we finished the third extra mandated chorus, she dove off the table into the outstretched arms of her admiring audience. They stood her upright; she raised her hand, pointed to the bar and yelled, "Another round on 'my movie star'!"

I'm not an expert on show business by any means, but I'm almost certain that I'd be correct in saying that performers are not supposed to drink beer while putting on their show. With a room full of my closest friends egging me on, I broke that rule pretty badly. I don't remember a lot about the later part of the evening. The last thing I remember clearly is playing the guitar and singing "Bad, Bad Leroy Brown" while leading a Conga line around the bar. I didn't have to worry about getting fired cause my boss Tom and his wife Debra were somewhere behind me in line. When the last song was played, there was thunderous applause and laughter.

Thank God Essie had the forethought to see the end of the evening approaching and didn't partake of the Devil's brew, so there was at least one car with a sober driver leaving Ratty's.

* * *

The sun seemed to be beating a hole in the side of *Last Dance*'s aft cabin and straight into my pounding brain. I covered up my eyes with a pillow in a last ditch effort to sleep it off.

"Okay, Cappy, here's your coffee. Rise and shine. That was quite the party last night. I met a lot of your friends that I hadn't known before. A pretty wild bunch for a semi-geriatric crowd."

"I don't think they're that old."

"There was an awful lot of silver hair in the group."

"Too much time in the sun. Damn, my head is killing me."

"Here's some aspirin with your coffee. Finish your first cup and get your pants on. We've got company onboard."

"Who?"

"Grimshaw."

"You're kidding."

"Nope. Come on. He's already up in the cockpit."

I drug my aching body topside.

"Good morning, Cappy. Appreciate you're letting me crash here last night. If Essie hadn't driven me home with you guys, I'd probably be passed out in my rental car in New Bern. That was quite the soiree last night. Our world famous Hollywood parties ain't got nothing on you guys."

"What are you doing back here? I thought you had a lot of things going on back on the left coast."

"I'm taking a little sabbatical. Besides, after my trip down the coast with you and Miss Essie, I've decided to make some changes in my lifestyle."

"And they would be?"

"I bought a boat."

"You're kidding."

"Nope. Bought a Morgan 45 ketch. It's right down the road in Fairfield Harbor at Northwest Creek Marina. She's a beauty. Needs a little cosmetic upgrading but I want to help with that. And there's another thing."

"You're full of surprises this morning. What else are you up to?"

"I've got a new love in my life and she loves sailing. When I tell her *The Lone Ranger* – that's what I'm calling the boat – is ready to go, she's going to fly out here and we, being me, her, and you and Essie are going to sail out to the island you raved about so much."

"You mean Ocracoke?"

"That's the place. What do you say?"

"It's fine with me. What do you say to that, Essie?"

"Hey, I love Ocracoke as much as you do. We could go this coming Sunday if your boat is ready for a trip that quick."

"I'll get her ready. I can hire a couple of guys at the marina to help me work on her and I'll call Sara right now and get her on a plane."

"Sara, huh?"

"She's a doll. We've known each other for several years. I was not thinking clearly in the female department. I was always going out with these twenty year olds with stars in their eyes and not much behind them. Sara, well, she's a lot like me. She's ready for a change too. If she likes the boat and sailing, hell, we might just take off for the Caribbean."

"Jim, you're an impulsive rascal, aren't you?"

"I knew after two days on *Calypso* that I needed a lot more of that. And I missed you guys too. Now, tell me how in world you pulled off getting another boat so soon. Did you win the lottery or something?"

"It's a good story. Let me get some toast and another coffee and I'll tell you the whole tale. It was mostly luck."

Essie shook her pretty head. "It was not luck. It was just what was supposed to happen. I don't know what it will take to get him to understand how things work."

"Essie, thanks for putting me in the back seat and bringing me home with you guys last night. The last thing I need is some bad publicity."

"No problem, Jim. You want a refill?"

"Might as well. Cappy is going to tell me the entire *Last Dance* story so I'll probably be here for a while."

"It's a good one. When you're ready to head back into town, let me know and I'll give you a ride."

"Will do. When we go, maybe you and Cappy can come see my boat."

"I'm sure Cappy would love the opportunity. I know I'm anxious to see her. Did you meet Stu and Shelia or Lou and Helen last night?"

"I think I met everybody at your table. Lou and Helen are the couple that's living on their boat, right?"

"That's them. Maybe they'd like to go to Ocracoke on their boat too. We could turn it into a group cruise. They're a lot of fun."

"Go ahead and ask them. I'll have the boat ready. Count on it. And if I don't…"

"Yes, you and Sara can come with us."

"You read my mind. But I'm sure I'll have the boat ready."

Jim stayed through lunch, until my head quit hurting. We drove him into New Bern, about thirty miles from SeaGate Marina. *The Lone Ranger* was a large boat. It was an older Morgan, but massively built with a good reputation as a cruising boat. He had described it accurately. It needed a lot of varnish, paint, and elbow grease but appeared to be sound. The motor ran good and the sails seemed to be decent.

"Jim, I think you'll be ready to go on the trip on this boat."

"I'm counting on it. Sara will get in late tonight and we'll be ready to go shortly after that. You're going to call your friends?"

"I already spoke with Lou and Helen; they're a go. The Stovalls have just bought a small boat. Essie and I are going to go to check it out before we leave town and see if they are interested. I'll give you a call on your cell phone and coordinate meeting up with you on the river."

"I'm excited. This is more fun than a premiere party."

"I'll have to take your word on that."

6

The start of this trip had ominous overtones. A cold front was coming through. In late January, that can mean pretty cold temperatures in North Carolina. The latest forecast showed rain moving in as well. But everyone loved Ocracoke; the boats were up to it with fully enclosed cockpits and heaters, so the executive decision was made to continue on. Larry and Linda Jo on *Island Time* and Darlene and Martin on *Great Scot* decided to come along as well. That would make for a great time on the magical little island.

We shoved off around eight a.m. as it was about a seven hour trip. It was agreed that Grimshaw would leave New Bern around six in the morning and join us on the Neuse as we approached from Adam's Creek. To our surprise, just as the creek emptied into the Neuse, we saw *The Lone Ranger* under genny and mizzen – probably the diesel as well – aiming straight for our fleet. She was an impressive sight. Her hull and rig were large and in spite of her weight, she seemed to move quickly through the water. *Zephyr* and the Stovall's new boat, a small Hunter named *Imagine*, spread out from the group and took their own heading toward the other side of the Pamlico Sound. The Pamlico is a large body of water, seventy miles long and over thirty miles wide. When you're in the middle of it, there's no view of land and it has a reputation for getting snotty in a blow.

Ocracoke was almost due east from the Neuse. Being a much smaller vessel with inexperienced crew, Darlene and Martin's boat *Great Scot*, a Beneteau First 28.5, fell in behind us for their first long cruise. *The Lone Ranger* moved over to our starboard and fell in behind Larry and Linda Jo on *Island Time*. There was a nice breeze on our stern quarter though the sky was very overcast and there was a humid chill to the air.

All was going smoothly. As we approached the NR marker indicating the mouth of the Neuse where it empties into the Pamlico Sound, Essie noticed a sailboat to our port that was far too close to the shoals at Maw Point. Many boats had gone aground there. I recognized the boat as belonging to a friend from New Bern. Everyone already knows this story in our circle and their embarrassment has been lasting. They are Jim and Joanie and their boat, a Catalina 32, is *Airisall*. This was their first boat and they had no prior experience that I knew of. I called to them on the VHF to see if they were aware of their proximity to the shoal.

"*Airisall*, this is *Last Dance*. Do you copy?"

I called them several times before I got a reply in a rather anguished tone. "Go ahead *Last Dance*. This is *Airisall*."

I asked them to switch to a working channel to leave the hailing channel sixteen clear.

"Jim, where are you guys headed?"

"We're on our way to Ocracoke. We're headed to the NR marker right now."

"I'm afraid you're not, Jim. You're headed to NR Junction, which is not the same marker. If you keep heading to NR Junction from where you are now, you're going to run straight over the shoals at Maw Point where it's only 2 foot deep."

"You're kidding. There's two NR markers?"

"Sort of. They're different but they both have NR in their name."

"What heading do we need to take to go to NR?"

"Give me a minute and I'll get you a rough bearing."

I approximated where they were and took a heading from the chart.

"Jim, you need to run at least a 170 degree heading to make NR."

"Thanks, Les. You saved my butt. I owe you."

"No problem, Jim. See you in Ocracoke."

We continued on toward NR and were astonished to look back at *Airisall* and see that she was headed completely opposite from the course I had given them.

"*Airisall*, this is *Last Dance*. Switch to a working channel." I continued, "Yes, *Airisall*. Did you decide against going to Ocracoke?"

"No. We're heading toward NR right now."

"You're 180 degrees off the course I gave you."

"That can't be, I'm looking at the compass right now."

The light finally went off my head. "Jim, you're looking at the numbers on the wrong side of your compass. Look at the far side, to where the arrow is pointing."

"Damn, this is embarrassing."

"Not to worry, Jim. Look, if you're going to Ocracoke, why not just fall in behind *Great Scot* who's tailing us? You'll be right on course and if you have a problem, we'll be close by."

"Great idea. We're headed toward you now."

I shudder to think what could have happened if we hadn't come along at the right moment.

As we continued across the Sound, the sky grew greyer and darker. The wind began to increase and it was apparent the predicted cold front was making its appearance. A light rain began to fall. Dark areas of heavier rain started filling in behind us. Before long we were in a torrential rain. Some muffled thunder came from back in the clouds. Since we were the mother goose in the parade I felt it was necessary to tighten up the formation.

"*Great Scot* and *Airisall*, you might want to pull up tighter behind us since it's raining so hard. We can barely make you out back there. Also, I wouldn't touch anything metal if I could avoid it."

Martin came back with his problem, "You mean like my wheel?"

"Exactly. Just go to your autopilot."

"It's not working."

"Okay, then just have Darlene stay away from you as much as possible and keep the barbecue sauce handy."

"I don't think that's funny."

"You're right. Very insensitive. I'm sure you'll be fine but both of you stay tight enough behind us so that you can see where we're going if this storm gets worse. The GPS has quit reading for the moment. I think there's too much interference. I've gotten out a chart and I'll keep a dead reckoning for my heading so stay with me."

"Will do."

None of the other boats were visible so I gave them all a call on the radio. They were fine. *The Lone Ranger* had jumped in close behind *Island Time* and Lou and Stuart were only fifty feet apart. Everyone had furled their sails and were motoring through the

Sound. As quickly as it came, the front moved through and left a light breeze and clearing sky. Three hours later the little fleet entered the Big Foot Channel and thirty minutes after that we were all secure at anchor in Silver Lake at Ocracoke.

Within a half hour of securing the boats, everyone was ready for a double-decker, greasy old cheeseburger from the Jolly Roger. The Jolly Roger is Ocracoke's most notorious hamburger joint. The atmosphere can't be beat. It's literally built over the water on pilings in Silver Lake. A large wooden picnic table was commandeered on the corner of the deck. A local band was setting up on the small bandstand. With their long beards and blue-collar worker outfits they looked like rejects from a *Grateful Dead* look-a-like contest. Their first song erased any doubts as to their ability to turn a song, and before long the place was jumping. The burgers hit the spot as did the constant influx of beer pitchers for the guys and margaritas for the gals. Essie and I loved this place. She leaned over and laid her head on my shoulder.

"The Bahamas or Ocracoke, I don't care. As long as we can be together like this I'm in heaven. I hope I don't ever wake up from this dream."

"You are the answer to most of my dreams. I'd hoped we'd be in the Keys by now, but this ain't bad."

After a couple hours of music and libations, the conversation focused on *Airisall*'s problems with the compass during the trip over. Lou figured he had come up with the answer.

"Jim, I know what happened on *Airisall* today."

"You do, Lou? Why am I afraid to ask what the answer is?"

"It's very simple. A construction issue?"

"How do you figure that?"

"It's just logic on my part. Stick with me now. Your boat was installed improperly under the compass. It was accidentally mounted ass backwards making your compass read in reverse!"

The place erupted with laughter. Jim and Joanie were good sports and we all knew he would be cataloguing this abuse and God help Lou if he ever gave Jim the chance to get on his case. And that opportunity always comes back around.

About two in the morning, the Jolly Roger determined that their employees needed sleep. Our little group of about fourteen desperate souls walked back to the dinghy docks for the late night ride back to our individual boats. The sun had been down for hours and we were now closer to the sunrise. Essie and I decided to sit up in the cockpit for a while and enjoy the moment. I looked over at her sitting there with the moonlight bouncing off the quiet water before it illuminated her beautiful face. There was a new reality in my life of fantasy. I had run away from many things thinking that if I had no entanglements in my life I'd be happier. I knew now I was wrong. Being involved is the best thing that can happen to a person. It's just that the person you're involved with has to be the right person. When I finally gave up on all things of that sort, they found me. I knew that as farfetched as the idea may have seemed just a few months earlier, I was in love, really in love. Essie was who I had needed all along. I wanted more than just a pretty face to look at. I wanted someone who shared my passion for adventure, someone who would not be so driven to arrange a secure stay in the nursing home for the last few years of life that they quit living during the best years of their life. She was there with me now. I threw my arm around her and determined that whatever it took, I'd make her days happy and full of love and living. We'd find the path to our own paradise, wherever that might wind up being. That night we both felt something different as we lay in our bunk together in the aft cabin. I think it was that evening that we both knew we'd be spending the rest of our lives together. It was the best feeling I had ever experienced. It also meant a little more direction would be needed from then on. But I'd worry about that after the sun came up. Tonight, holding her was all that really mattered.

After the long trip across the Pamlico Sound to Ocracoke and the even longer evening singing and telling lies with friends, we slept in. There is nothing better than sleeping on a boat. The slight motion of the waves creates just enough movement to rock you to sleep. We were both snoring I'm sure, for Essie that would be a light purr, when a knock on the hull woke us.

"Who the heck could that be?"

"Okay, you guys, wake up. I've been bragging to Sara about your pancakes for weeks now and we're here to mooch breakfast off you."

"It's Grimshaw. Should we pretend we don't hear him and try to keep sleeping?"

"You think a ploy like that will work on him? Get real. We might as well get the oven going. Okay, Jim. Give us a minute to get some clothes on."

"Sounds good. We'll be waiting in the cockpit. And get that coffee going, would you?"

"Okay, okay, we're on it."

Essie threw on some blue jeans and a sweater while I struggled to just get my eyes open and use the head. By the time I finally drug myself up to the cockpit, she had already fixed everyone a cup of coffee and even had mine sitting on the cockpit table.

"Morning, Jim. And hello again, Sara. Sorry we didn't get to talk very much last night. Seemed like the music and beer kind of took over the whole evening."

"It was just lovely. I don't know when I've had that much fun. I really wanted to meet you, Essie. Jim has gone on about the two of you so much this past couple of weeks that I feel like I already know you. Anyway, it's certainly a pleasure to finally meet you. And Ocracoke is just spectacular."

"It is, Sara. Essie and I love it here. If the water was clear and it was eighty degrees all year, we wouldn't even want to go cruising. This would be all we'd want. And Jim, update us on how you are liking the Morgan 45 ketch."

"Well, after spending time on *Calypso*, I just couldn't resist the urge to get back on board a boat. I wanted my own where I could come and go anytime. I think Sara likes her as well."

"I do."

"What's not to like? Geez, she's a battleship. What's her displacement?"

"Around seventeen tons. She feels it too. In a four-foot chop she just slips right through it like a hot knife through butter as the saying goes."

"I'm sure she does. What are you going to do with her?"

"We don't have any concrete plans yet. We might just keep her in New Bern and come visit between films. I love just hanging out at marinas. I must be part wharf rat."

"I'm with you there."

"Now Cappy, what are you and Essie up to?"

"Well, we're just trying to survive my divorce and start cruising again. Right now we're keeping the wolf away singing at Captain Ratty's in New Bern. So many of our sailing friends hang out there. It's actually fun but I don't think we'll be able to make enough money there to get the boat fixed up and get back to sailing. I don't know what the answer is right now. Something will come up, I hope. If not, I guess we'll just clean boat bottoms. To be honest, we are about out of money. I don't see how it's going to be possible to fix up this old boat, get our cruising kitty back to the point we can go cruising or actually keep clothes on our back. Other than that, we're doing great. I don't know what the road ahead holds for us. Any suggestions? You know, a lot of folks have indicated they think I look like Robert Redford."

"They did, huh? These are folks you trust?"

"I detect a little cynicism there, don't I?"

"I just don't see a close resemblance. I could be wrong. The camera doesn't lie. Maybe you need a screen test. Now, I can see a little Telly Savalis there."

"Thanks a million."

"Hey, he's huge."

"Yeah, and bald with a nose as big as my fist."

"Now that you mention it, that is what I'm seeing."

"Wise ass. Ready for my world famous pancakes?"

"Aye, aye, Cappy."

After a mega-breakfast, the girls stayed down below and chatted in the cabin while Jim and I moved back to the cockpit with a fresh cup of coffee.

"Is that a little shot of Irish Crème I'm tasting?"

"I believe you're right, Jim. Pretty great stuff."

"You know, Les, I think I may have a solution for your employment situation. A way you could make money working in spurts and then go cruising between jobs?"

"That would be fantastic. What kind of work are you thinking about?"

"How would you like working on motion pictures, you know, movies?"

"That would be incredible, but how could I do that? I don't have any experience that would lend itself to getting that sort of job."

"Remember I told you this, Les. You'll laugh about it in a few years. The film business is all about two things, networking and nepotism and the latter is the prime mover. Almost everyone in the film business is either related to or somehow connected to somebody that got them started. It's been that way as long as I can remember, probably always has been that way."

"You'd help me get a job?"

"I would. I have a friend named Jeff Ginn who's been an art director in the movies for years. He's a great guy and I think you and he'd get along really well. I read in the *Hollywood Reporter* that he's getting ready to film a movie right down the road in Wilmington. If you're sure you want to try this, I'll give him a call and set up an interview for you."

"Jim, I'd be forever in your debt. How's the money in that business?"

"You'll make more in six months than you would in a year or even two years in a regular job. Of course, since it's non-union in this area, there's no benefits, no retirement, nothing. Just a great paycheck."

"Right now, that's the thing Essie and I need the most."

"It's a deal then. When we get back to New Bern, I'll make the call. I also have a check here for you and the missus."

"What check is that?"

"I want to cover the damage I did to the dock in St. Augustine. It was my fault and I want to make it good. It's not that much money to me right now and I know it would be somewhat of a help to you guys."

"Jim, I can't tell you how much this will help us."

"Not a problem. Now, what are we going to do out here today?"

"Let's just walk the little back streets. Essie loves the white sand paths and houses that look like they're out of a Norman Rockwell painting. Then we can come back to the Pelican for peel-and-eat shrimp for lunch. After that, well, sitting around in the cockpit with friends ain't too shabby either."

"Let's get on with it, shall we?"

7

I had been a movie buff all my life. Saturday mornings in Newport News, where I grew up, were spent at the small theatre in Hilton Village, about an hour's bike ride from my house. Usually, a buddy and I would get up early and make the trip in time to watch the Saturday morning cartoons followed by a double feature. More often than not, it was a classic western and a Three Stooges comedy. I could spend the entire day staring up at the silver screen imagining I was anywhere other than where I was. When I hit my teens, already a sailboat fanatic, I was mesmerized by Gardner McKay in "Adventures in Paradise." He was the captain of an eighty-four foot John Alden schooner named *Tiki* and affectionately called the *Leaky Tiki*. It was a majestic old boat and the South Pacific Islands he visited each week created fantasies in my imagination that have stayed with me to this day. Movies and television fueled my dreams like nothing else. The thought of actually working on a movie had my motor running.

The DEG studio was located on 23rd Street, better known as Airport Road in Wilmington, North Carolina. It was founded by Italian movie mogul Dino DeLaurentis shortly after he filmed "Firestarter" in the area. It struck him that North Carolina, as a right-to-work state with a low cost of doing business, would be the perfect place to build a studio. He could mass produce movies there at a fraction of the cost of Los Angeles or New York. He brought in top craftsman from all over the world and built a state-of-the-art complex where multiple films could be produced simultaneously. As I walked in the front door, I could feel the excitement just looking at the framed movie posters on the wall of the lobby. A young woman at the front desk asked my name and business there. I told her I was to meet a gentleman named Jeff Ginn, a friend of Grimshaw's who was expecting me. I don't know what I was expecting but Jeff certainly didn't fit the mold of a motion picture Art Director. He was six foot six inches tall, with a dark complexion and a Fu Manchu moustache. He smiled ear to ear as he offered me his hand. "You must be Les Pendleton. I'm Jeff."

"Nice to meet you, Jeff. I have to tell you I'm in awe to actually be in a movie studio. I've always been a movie fanatic."

"Everyone our age is, Les. It's in our DNA. I've been working in the industry for years and I'm still enamored of the process. Follow me and we'll take a quick tour of the lot."

"Lead on."

We walked through a maze of offices with dozens of people scurrying about with an obvious sense of urgency to their step. I could see in the offices that the staff was mostly young people, in their twenties and generally dressed like they were getting ready to mow the grass with shorts, sandals, headbands, and beards. They were pretty scraggly looking to my way of thinking. Most of the office spaces were divided into cubicles and the walls were covered with drawings of every imaginable topic. There were space ships, aliens, jungles, exotic cars, you name it. I followed Jeff as he turned into one large room filled with drafting tables. He walked over to the corner where the largest such table sat, covered with drawings and surrounded with props.

"This is my little part of the world, Les. I'm working on a Stephen King movie titled *Cat's Eye*. It's a series of three short stories that Stephen wrote. One of them needs a large, electrical sign built that can do some special things. Grimshaw told me that you were very experienced with these things."

"I am. My soon to be ex-father-in-law owns a large sign company in Jacksonville, North Carolina, and I worked for him a number of years. It was slave labor but I did learn everything you ever wanted to know about signs. What sort of special things is it that this sign is supposed to do?"

"The star gets caught with the bad guy's wife in their penthouse apartment at the top of a skyscraper. He escapes through a window and tries to move around the roof on a ledge. This large sign is in his way so he attempts to crawl over it. It looks like he might just make it, but then the plastic sign face falls forward with a ton of sparks coming out of it. It hangs open twenty floors up and our guy fights his way through all the electric sparks and flames. He hangs from it and slowly inches his way to the other side. He finally makes it. I need someone to build this sign to my specs. Does this sound like something you could do?"

"Basically, yes. In my sleep. I'd love to do it."

"How much would you charge me to do it?"

In all honesty, I didn't have a clue what to tell the man. I'd never made much money. My business sense was pathetic and the years at Carolina Bible Manufacturing were riddled with poverty. If I had made a little more money, been more successful, my first marriage might not have ended so painfully. Money, or rather the lack of it, had always been a subject of great controversy at our house. I assumed that folks making movies made a lot more money than I was used to so I threw out a number I thought he might spring for that would help Essie and I get the boat going and refill our cruising kitty. "How about seven hundred and fifty bucks a week?"

Without a blink Jeff replied, "How about fifteen hundred?"

"That's a lot more than I was expecting."

"Trust me, Les. You'll earn it. This is not an easy business. There's lots of huge egos, deadlines, assholes, and screw-ups. You'll probably think fifteen hundred isn't enough after thirty days. So, you on board?"

"Absolutely!"

"Wonderful. You're hired. How about I finish showing you the studio, especially the back lot? There's several movies being filmed here right now and if you've never seen one in production, you'll probably get a kick out of it."

"I'd love that."

In only a matter of days, I discovered I'd initially offered my services at approximately half the going rate for even carpenters on a movie. Fifteen hundred a week was entry level, the story of my life.

We walked out the back door of the main studio administrative building to what appeared to be a giant paved parking lot with six huge metal buildings sprinkled about on it. Jeff described for me which movies were in production in each building. At one we waited until a small light just outside the studio door turned from red to green and we entered.

"We're filming in here right now. This segment of the movie is about a gremlin, not much bigger than a rabbit, that is living in a little girl's room. Of course, our gremlin is a full-size person so we had to make a room about five times the normal size including everything in it. What do you think?"

It was astounding. The room looked perfect other than being immense in size. It had a rocking chair you would need a ten-foot tall extension ladder to get up on. The bed looked like a basketball court and there was even a golf ball about five feet in diameter in one corner. In another corner was what looked to be a huge ball of tangled string.

"What's that?"

"A dust ball. Pretty neat, huh?"

I was like a kid in a candy shop as we looked around the lot. I was excited just thinking about the things I would see working here. "When do you want me to get started?"

"Last week. You'll find that movies are more about getting things done in a hurry and accurately than anything else. Producers care more about that than money most of the time. It costs about thirty-five thousand dollars an hour to film a movie as the cameras are running. So, anything less than that amount of money that saves them an hour is a good deal in their mind. I'm not sure I agree with that, but that's pretty much how it is. Can you be here first thing in the morning to get going on this sign?"

"I'll be here by seven."

"I'm looking forward to working with you, Les. Any friend of Grimshaw's..."

The studio was at least an hour and a half drive from SeaGate Marina. I could care less. I now had a job that I would enjoy and make enough money that Essie and I could continue working toward our dream of fixing up *Last Dance* and heading south by the following winter. When I got back to the boat I couldn't contain my joy over the day's events. Lou and Helen came aboard and we all celebrated until about eight thirty. I knew the next day would come early so Essie and I turned in by nine p.m. We celebrated once more by exploring our respective danger zones and then collapsing into a deep sleep. The alarm seemed to go off five minutes after I fell asleep. Essie awoke with me and fixed me a quick cup of coffee and a warmed up pastry for the road. She gave me a huge hug as I got ready to leave.

"Cappy, this could be what we've been looking for. I hope you have the best day ever. Enjoy every minute. I'll be here working on the boat. There's a help-wanted sign in the marina window and I'm going to check on that this morning. I'd love to make a few dollars too. The more we make the quicker we can escape."

I kissed her and almost jogged to the car. The drive went by quickly as I spent iy contemplating my approach to building the movie sign. It didn't seem that complicated to me and I felt very confident I could give them a good product. Jeff was friendly with me. He went out of his way to give me tips he thought would help with the project and was very approving of the sign as it came together. I had hired a young man named Tim to help me. He was a competent welder and had a very artistic side to him, even if he did look like Grizzly Adams. I knew there were several stars working on the lot but I was kinda isolated in the construction area and only occasionally got to go where any filming was taking place. It was therefore more than a little surprising one morning when Jeff came by my shop with a request.

"Les, you know the waters in this area, right? You said you were sailor."

"That's right. I know this whole coastal area very well."

"Have you ever done any fishing?"

"Tons. Years ago, a buddy and I went almost every day. I was working at a tackle shop shortly after I got out of school and in the mornings, before work, we would take a small skiff and go float fishing for king mackerel."

"That's great. Listen, one of the actors working on a movie here is an avid fisherman and he wants someone familiar with the area to take him out a few times. Would you be able to do that? If it doesn't make you late building the sign for me, I'll even pay you the days you take him so it doesn't cost you anything."

"Wow. That sounds too good to be true. Who is the actor? Anybody I've heard of?"

"I would imagine. It's Michael Keaton. You know, *Mr. Mom.*"

"You've got to be kidding. He's one of my all-time favorites. I loved him in "Nightshift." What's he filming here?"

"It's a low budget feature called "The Squeeze." He's the biggest star in it. Can you take a break for a while and let's go over to his honeywagon so I can introduce you."

"Absolutely. This is exciting. I mean I know Grimshaw pretty well but he's not nearly as big a star as Michael Keaton."

"Well, I wouldn't tell Jim that. You know, actors and their egos."

"To me, Jim is the brightest star in Hollywood. Without him I wouldn't even be here. But, Michael Keaton. Essie will flip out when she hears this."

We walked a short way across the studio lot to a side street where the honeywagons were parked. They are basically just nice RVs that the production company rents for the stars to relax in when they are not needed on the set. We walked up to one and Jeff knocked on the door.

"Anybody home?"

"Hey Jeff, come on in."

Sitting at the dinette table in the small RV was a face I'd recognize anywhere. He smiled warmly and held out his hand. "You must be Les. I understand you are quite the fisherman."

"Maybe not the best you'll find but I've certainly done a lot of it around here. I used to run a tackle shop on the beach and I've fished this coast a lot. It's a real pleasure to meet you. Without embarrassing you or myself, I'm a fan. And my kids love you."

"That's the story of my career. Clooney gets all the women and I get the kids! Just kidding. I'm thankful for every one of them that ever bought a ticket to see me. Come on in and let's talk fishing."

He was genuinely warm and friendly. Jeff excused himself and left us to talk. Within a minute it was like two guys who both liked to fish were just talking shop. There was no movie star in the room. I liked him from the moment we met. We set up a time to go fishing in the ocean the following week. I had a friend with a nice sport fisherman I knew would be thrilled to take him out. He normally took charters but to take Michael Keaton on his boat would be a gratis trip. The film Michael was working on was about half done. It co-starred Rae Dawn Chong and the rocker, Meatloaf. It was definitely a B flick but Michael was an A actor in my book.

Jeff had spread my name around on the lot and several of the other shows that were filming there had called me for work, including Michael's. We worked the day and evening before our fishing trip until almost midnight. The arrangements were made that Michael would get up at four a.m., drive north to Jacksonville, North Carolina, and I'd meet him there. I'd drive the rest of the way to Emerald Isle where my friend's boat was berthed. I was in the parking lot where we arranged to meet at five a.m. Michael pulled in precisely on time. I could see on his face that he nose was "draggin' in the dirt" as the saying goes.

"Les, if you don't mind, I'm exhausted. I'm going to shut my eyes and take a nap while you drive us the rest of the way."

"No problem. I'll wake you when we get there."

It was extremely early and Mike didn't stir for the next forty-five minutes as I drove to the coast. It was hard to believe that here I was, basically in the middle of nowhere, taking a well-known movie star fishing. It was also interesting to look over and see this unshaven guy with a familiar face, lower jaw hanging open and snoring as I drove. Life can be very strange at times. As we arrived at Emerald Isle, a small beach town in the middle of the state, I woke Mike up to tell him we were there.

"Great, I feel a little better now that I've had a full four hours of sleep. But we're going fishing and that makes it all worthwhile. Say, I'm starving. I didn't get anything to eat before I left this morning and I know I can't get out on the ocean on a boat with nothing in my stomach. Is there anywhere around here we can grab a quick bite of something?"

"There's a small deli right where we turn in to the marina. That's about all that's open here this early. I'm not sure they'll have much other than donuts this time of day."

"Some donuts will be fine with me. Let's do it."

We turned into the empty parking lot of the small shopping area. It was basically a little strip mall with about four stores. The K&V Deli was the only place open. When we entered, we discovered only the cashier was there, a young girl, perhaps sixteen years old. We walked over to the counter in front of her that had a glass front and contained several varieties of fresh donuts. The young woman was apparently glad to have some company and smiled broadly at us.

"Good morning! You guys going fishing this morning?"

"That's right. How did you guess?"

"No one but fishermen are ever here this early. The marina is at the end of the street about a block away. We see a lot of them."

Mike pointed to a nice apple-filled pastry and asked her for a couple. As she grabbed a napkin and picked them up to place in a bag she continued chatting with us. "Guess what?"

Mike was very friendly with her. "What?"

"My boyfriend is taking the famous actor Michael Keaton fishing this morning."

Mike never batted an eye as he replied. "You've got to be kidding. Do you think if we are at the marina this morning we'll get to meet him?"

"You probably will. It's a small boatyard. But look, don't go down there and make assholes out of yourselves. You'll get my boyfriend fired. He wasn't supposed to let anybody know he would be there."

Mike, still poker faced looked her right in the eye and made the zipped lip gesture. "Mums the word. We won't say a thing. By the way, what's your boyfriend's name?"

"Eric. Why?"

"Just wanted to see what kind of guy is dating such a pretty young woman."

She blushed and though staring *Mr. Mom* straight in the face from less than two feet away, she never figured it out. I was trying my best to not start laughing out loud. Of course, as soon as we arrived at the boat and I introduced Michael to everyone, he immediately went over to the first mate, Eric, and related what had just happened. Everyone had a good laugh. I told Michael the poor girl would probably slit her wrists when Eric told her that evening what she had done.

It was a beautiful day on the ocean. The water was calm and deep blue. We motored swiftly to a good spot and the captain slowed the boat down to a good trolling speed. "Okay, Mike. Bait's out. Get comfortable and when something strikes, we'll hand you the rod."

"That's great. I'm excited."

Less than a minute later the rod started singing as the drag started to play out with a large fish on the line. Eric grabbed the rod from the holder and handed it to Michael who sat down in the fighting chair in the center of the cockpit. He had a good size king mackerel on the line. It took a couple of minutes to bring it in and when he finally boarded it, he picked it up and raised it in the air over his head like an Indian Chief might raise an offering to the Great Spirit in the sky. I took the opportunity to snap a couple of pictures of the event. He didn't seem to mind. As the morning continued the fish cooperated and before long he had boated about four nice fish. About this time, with the crew in great spirits, Michael got a phone call on his cell phone. He stepped up to the boat's flying bridge to get away from the noise so he could hear better. Everyone on the boat could still hear his end of the conversation. It went something like this.

"I can't, Katy. I've got some problems on the contract I'm not happy with and I'm not going to come in this morning until it gets worked out. I'm not trying to be a pain about this but that's just how I feel. No, I'm at the house, why?"

At just that moment, a rod sang out with a large fish on, and the captain yelled to Michael, "Fish on, Mike."

Michael looked at the bent double fishing rod, looked back at the phone, looked again at the rod, bouncing hard with the large fish attached to the end of the line. In an almost comic manner he hit the shut off button on the phone and dropped it into the helmsman seat on the boat's bridge. He jumped down into the fighting chair and played the large fish until he had it on the floor of the cockpit. Meanwhile, his phone had rung several more times. He wiped the fish juice off his hands and went back up to the phone. It quickly rang again and this time he took the call.

"Yeah, sorry Katy. Got a bad connection out here at the house. I'll start heading that way pretty soon. I'll call in about an hour and let you know where I'm at. I have to get dressed and everything."

Fishing with Michael Keaton

Michael came down to us and said, "Guys, as much fun as this has been, I have to go back to work this afternoon. I've had a ball and I can't tell you how much I appreciate you doing this for me."

I was very impressed. In spite of all his success and fame, he was still just a good guy, one like I had hoped he would be. He remained very friendly to me for the entire time he was in the Wilmington area filming and, to this day, I have nothing but good things to say about Michael Keaton. One thing I have noticed over the years, having now worked on many films is the special sort of relationships that actors and actresses make while filming a movie. Many are very friendly and even want to be involved socially with locals. They uniformly say, "Be sure to give me a call sometime if you're on the west coast" or "We'll work together on my next film; I'll ask for you." All I can say is, don't hold your breath. You have to remember that they are having their butts kissed 24/7 and don't live in the real world. I'm sure their phone is ringing nonstop from "old friends" trying to get up with them later. Once they have moved on, you're wasting your time to try and get in contact with them. You have to remember: They're famous and you're not. You are not on the same playing field and there is almost nothing you can do for them that needs doing that isn't already being done. Just get over it.

8

The film business was turning out to be just what the doctor ordered for Essie and me. I would work extremely hard for the length of time it took to film a movie, usually about ninety days. The pay was the best I'd ever made and it was giving us the funds we needed to get *Last Dance* in cruising condition. I didn't like the amount of time we were apart but we were both working toward our goal of setting sail. Essie was working in the marina office checking boats in and out and working the cash register. The office was like a small convenience store with a lot of items that cruisers and fishermen need. They also sold gas and diesel fuel on the dock. Essie got to greet all the cruising sailors and she was a natural fit for the job. Everyone there loved her just as I did. She would talk to all the cruisers about where they were going, where they had been, and anything else that was interesting. When I got home at night we'd share the day's events and savor the evening hours together. Essie had been nothing but supportive and we were growing closer by the day. Grimshaw left to film a movie in Charlotte named "Days of Thunder" that starred Tom Cruise and Robert Duval. He made no bones about how much he was looking forward to working on such a mega production. I was extremely grateful to Jim for his help in getting me the movie job and the subsequent work it led to. Little did I know that in the coming years I'd be working with Tom Cruise myself and many other actors I enjoyed watching on the silver screen. Movie work would be the funding we needed for our escape ticket to paradise. We could work four months and then take our savings and go sailing.

With Tom Cruise while filming "Billy Bathgate"

We would be leaving early summer for the Bahamas. My heart raced every time I even thought about it. From talking to other folks working on films, they were out of work about as much as they worked. For them, while raising kids and paying bills, it was not the ideal solution. For Essie and me, it was perfect. I didn't realize it at the time but I had just followed a different path down the road of life. In looking back, I'm not even sure how it all came about but I was now much closer to living a life that fit me than I had ever dreamed possible. I was in love with Essie, and we seemed to be a perfect match. I was working at something I truly enjoyed and making more money doing it than I had while doing something I hated, only to make a buck. I was starting to believe there was a greater power that helps us make changes if we really want to make them.

Though fundamentally sound, *Last Dance* needed a lot of work. I had learned long ago that you should expect everything on an old boat to need to be repaired or upgraded. A forty-three foot, ocean worthy sailboat has a ton of systems on it. There is a diesel engine, batteries, an alternator on the engine to charge the batteries, and a charger that works when the boat is connected to shore power. There is a fresh water system for showering and doing the dishes. There's another fresh water system that cools the engine. There are two complete electrical systems: one that runs on twelve volts or battery power, and another that runs on 110 volts when the shore power is connected. There are two toilets, each with its own intake for water to assist flushing and a holding tank to contain the waste until it can be pumped out at a marina with the proper facilities to handle it. There is central heat and A/C, a propane system for the oven and also refrigeration. On top of all this is the rigging, sails, mast, deck hardware, topside canvas, and the list goes on and on. *Last Dance* desperately needed to have all of these systems checked out and brought up to dependable condition. It would not be good to have any of these essential systems fail at sea. On top of all of this, she needed to be pulled at a boat yard to have the bottom checked and a couple of coats of bottom paint applied. All of this would be costly, even if Essie and I did the work ourselves. Nonetheless, with an overly optimistic outlook, we pulled *Last Dance* and began the tedious process of refurbishing her. It wouldn't be to bristol condition but we would at least get her to the point that we felt she could take us where we wanted to travel and feel like she was up to the task. Once we had her on the hard, sitting in the boat yard on stands, we could see that she had years of bottom paint buildup on her. She needed to be completely sanded to the gel coat and repainted. It was dirty, nasty work but we persevered. Lou Schroder had turned out to be one of the closest friends I'd ever had. He was from the old school. A self-made man, he was out of the mold of John Wayne and Teddy Roosevelt.

Lou and Cappy doing what they do best

Though dealing with a number of health issues including high blood pressure, he never slowed down and worked like a twenty-year-old every day. I would get on him sometimes to slow down and enjoy life but he couldn't stop working. He loved being on a boat of any size. He would drive a small powerboat pushing a barge one day and captain a two hundred foot ferry the next. We always joked that if they would let him wear a uniform, Lou would captain a bike. And to top it off, if you didn't want Lou's help on some nasty job you were doing, you'd have to hide. If there was work to be done, especially on a boat, Lou was always there to help his friends. You didn't need to ask. If you said you were going to start working at eight in the morning, by five minutes after eight, Lou would be there. Having owned a machine shop and prospered as an inventor, Lou was very talented with all things mechanical and nautical. He was a lot of help when working on a boat.

Essie worked side by side with me, finishing up the day covered with old paint and caulk but still able to smile and offer encouragement to me. I loved the optimism she brought to life. She was always positive and a lot of the time I wasn't. She was a great balancing weight to me. We would shower in the boatyard's old restroom and head back out to *Last Dance* to spend the night. We had a stepladder pulled up to her stern and we'd climb aboard and fall asleep in each other's arms until the alarm went off at daylight to start over again. This process continued on for a full six weeks. Though exhausted, our floating home was starting to look great and many of the repairs she needed had been completed. We were ready to put her back in the water. We were not going to go back to SeaGate however. By this time, Lou and Helen had moved *Zephyr* to New Bern and we were going to follow them. *Last Dance* would be back at Northwest Creek Marina where I used to keep *Calypso*. It would be somewhat like going home. We intended to keep working on the boat there for another two months and then take off for the Bahamas. Our plans were coming to fruition.

Our crew of friends had a ritual of sharing just about every evening in each others' cockpits as spring came into full bloom. When I wasn't working at the film studio, Tom Ballance would let me play a couple evenings a week at Captain Ratty's. That left a lot of time to complete the work on *Last Dance* and get ready to head south. One evening in the cockpit of *Zephyr*, we came to the decision that we needed to have an annual formal party to celebrate the arrival of summer. There was a restaurant in New Bern named the Chelsea that we all enjoyed. It was in a historic building in downtown New Bern that had at one time been a pharmacy where pharmacist Caleb Bradham, who invented of Pepsi-Cola worked. There was a luxurious banquet room upstairs that was decorated to honor the buildings 1800s origin. It could hold up to a hundred or so folks and they would serve a great meal to go with the party. The girls jumped right on it as it gave them the opportunity to get all dolled up and see what their men would look like if they ever got cleaned up. We all agreed it would be a nice change of format for one our parties and we'd do it as a trial that spring. If everyone had a good time, we could do it annually. The Chelsea would be a particularly good spot to hold it as there were at least two marinas close by where we could take our boats for the weekend. That would be especially good if someone, heaven forbid, had a little too much of the bubbly. They could walk back to their boats as opposed to getting in any type of vehicle on the highway. The ladies were extremely excited.

Over the next several days they covered every facet of party planning from what band to hire to place settings and table decorations. They were taking it very seriously. Of course, all the guys talked about was the fact they would have to rent a tuxedo. A couple of the guys said they would wear their dress uniforms from the service and Lou said he'd be wearing his Merchant Mariner's dress whites. I will admit to being a little excited about the evening myself.

The day of the formal party turned out to be spectacular. We left SeaGate Marina early in the morning and had a broad reach all the way up the Neuse River courtesy of the prevailing summer winds in the area, which blow almost constantly out of the southwest. Lou and Helen in *Zephyr* sailed alongside and the two boats held almost identical speeds the entire distance. With *Last Dance* being a Gulfstar and *Zephyr* being an Endeavour, the boats could easily be called cousins.

Cappy and Essie beside *Last Dance*

The factories that built them both were not only in the same city but also on the same street in St. Petersburg, Florida. The story goes that when one company was busier than the other, their employees often bounced between these two companies as well as among Irwin and Morgan Yachts which were also built there. There were many similarities in construction and materials. Today, both are considered to be heavy, well-built production boats that sail well and are seaworthy. They certainly weren't speed demons but offered a solid sense of security at sea.

I was never that interested in speed; I wanted a reasonable amount of performance and a lot of seaworthiness. Gulfstars were also known for a very sea-kindly motion in a seaway. We made a good six to seven knots all the way to New Bern. As we arrived, we could see several of our friends boats tied up to the transient dock at the Sheraton Grande Marina where we would all be spending the night.

There was a couple of hours to spare before we had to put on our monkey suits and walk the two blocks to the Chelsea. That meant there was time to gather on Lou's boat and have a couple of cold beers. Before long, *Zephyr* was at capacity with ten couples aboard laughing and enjoying the warm afternoon breeze. Lou had cranked up his favorite Willie Nelson album on the cockpit speakers. The ladies had gone below to the ship's galley and made a batch of "pain killers" to help them get in the mood for the serious partying that would take place throughout the evening. We were having such a good time at the dock that it was almost painful when the girls came topside and informed us it was time to transition into our James Bond attire.

Helen, Essie, and Shelia aboard *Last Dance*

As we entered the ballroom in the Chelsea, the band was already in place playing some great old standards from the era of the Rat Pack. Sinatra, Dean Martin, Sammy Davis Jr., and others of that era always got my juices flowing. The ladies had the room decorated to the nines and tables were set up for the ninety or so guests. Leigh Pfefferkorn was taking photos of each couple as they arrived. For most of us, I'm sure the chances of getting a picture of us in formal outfits were pretty limited. The girls weren't going to waste this opportunity to record the occasion. I have to admit that it was a regal affair and we wer all enjoying the formal ambiance. The food and company were first-rate.

Grimshaw attended with his Army dress blues on. Lou, as promised, was resplendent in his Mariner's dress whites. Some of the guys wore white dinner jackets and a few of the old traditionalists, such as me, wore the standard black tux with a black bow tie. We ate, danced, and mingled until the feet were tired, the stomachs were stretched, and the jaws needed rest. Everyone agreed it had been a special evening, worthy of an annual event. The girls booked the room again for the following year before we left that evening. Lou and Helen, Stuart and Shelia, Jim and Sara, and Miss Essie and I all walked together back to the marina. No one felt like turning in yet so we reconvened on *Last Dance* for a late night shot of Bailey's and a few moments of quieter conversation as we wound down for the night. Lou quizzed us on our plans.

"So, Les, when are you and Miss Essie heading south? You know it's late in the year to be heading in that direction? June 1st starts hurricane season. You won't be able to get insurance to cover you."

"Lou, not a problem. We don't have any insurance on the boat. If we lose it, we'll just be screwed. It's already happened to us once, not long ago if you'll recall. If we wait 'til we have the time and the money, we'll never go. We're hell-bent to get to the tropics and we're just going to do it. I wish you and Helen would take *Zephyr* and come along with us."

"I'm thinking about it. I'd like to take another cruise. It's been a couple of years since we've actually made a decent voyage. I love the Caribbean and the Bahamas, even in the summer. Let me sleep on it a couple of days and I'll let you know."

"What about you and Shelia, Stuart? You said you wanted to get a bigger boat and head out."

"We are getting a new boat, a forty-seven foot Stephens Custom offshore sloop. We will be leaving in the fall after I get the boat tricked out the way I want it."

"Spectacular! Where are you going?"

"I'm not saying where we'll wind up but I know we'll be heading toward the deep Caribbean, probably straight from Beaufort to St. Maarten. From there, we'll take it one day at a time. I don't know how long we're going to be gone or when we'll be back. My choice would be to sail around the world and spend five years doing it. But I have to have Shelia on board with the plan and she's a little more conservative about it than I am. So, we'll make those decisions in place."

"Geez, I'm jealous. I'm glad you're getting to do it but I don't see how we'll ever be ahead enough to do a trip like that. I'll be happy with the Bahamas."

"Les, you never know where life might take you. Just be bold and go for your dreams. Every trip starts with a single step. You don't take the first step, you'll never go anywhere."

Lou chimed in with a toast. "To good friends and sailing. The best of all things."

As the clock struck two a.m., we were all ready to crash. We saw that everyone got safely back to the docks then Essie and I slipped below and collapsed into our aft bunk. To be lying there with such a wonderful woman after having a grand evening with friends, I was acutely aware of how special the night had been. My life was in a much better place.

We all slept in late the next morning before gathering on Jim and Sara's boat, *The Lone Ranger* for pancakes and Bloody Marys. I could tell that Jim and Sara enjoyed the sailing crowd immensely.

"Well, Jim. It ain't a Hollywood party but what did you think?"

"Sara and I were talking about that just this morning while we were still in the sack. I don't know of any place I'd rather be or any people I'd rather spend time with than this group right here. I've only known most of you for a short while but I feel more of a real friendship with you guys than with folks I've known in California for decades. They don't seem real compared to the sailing crowd. I'm thinking about slowing down on my career some; I'm not a young man anymore. I think I'll at least split my time between working on location and here. New Bern is a wonderful little town. It's safe, clean, and has a lot of history. California, especially Los Angeles, is no place to live in my book. Crime, overcrowding, smog, bad values, and more fruitcakes than you'll find on the rest of the planet combined. I like it here a hell of a lot more. This is more like where I grew up in Georgia."

Though still officially springtime, it was unusually warm and you could feel the heat already building. Miss Essie and I wanted to get to Northwest Creek before too late in the day so we could adjust the lines on our new slip in that marina. We all headed back to our boats and started to prepare for the sail home. Once everything below was properly stowed, we cast off the dock lines and set off. We hadn't cleared the drawbridge in New Bern more than ten minutes before dark clouds started moving into the area. Essie looked at the sky and then over to me.

"Cappy, I can feel moisture in the air and the temperature is dropping. I'm willing to bet a thunderstorm isn't far off. We probably shouldn't even worry with putting up the sails if we're just going to have to secure them in a few minutes. Probably should just motor home. I'd like to get there before any storm hits."

"I'm all for that, too. Did Lou and the other boats make the bridge opening?"

"Nope. I think they're all staying at the Sheraton another night. It would have been nice to visit with everyone a little more but we've got a lot of work to do to get *Last Dance* ready."

"My thoughts exactly. It sure is getting dark."

It was about that time the marine VHF radio sounded out. "Mayday, mayday, U.S. Coast Guard, do you copy?"

It was not a correctly formatted call but the gist of it was pretty clear. Somebody was scared.

"This is Fort Macon Coast Guard. What is the nature of your problem?"

"We're not in trouble. I just wanted to report a really huge waterspout in the Neuse River. It's the biggest I've ever seen."

"Yes, sir. What is the location of the waterspout?"

"It's just upriver of the bridge in New Bern. It seems to be headed downriver."

"Yes, sir. Thank you for the report. We'll put out an alert. Coast Guard out."

Moments later, the Coast Guard made a general announcement and asked all vessels to be on the alert and report it if they saw it. Since we were smack in the center of the Neuse River, I was somewhat concerned. After ten or fifteen minutes there were no further alarms sounded so I was feeling a little less apprehensive, and then heard, "Mayday. Mayday. Coast Guard, we see the waterspout. It's huge with four little tornados dancing around the base of it."

"Yes, sir. What is the location of the waterspout? Can you tell what direction it's moving?"

"Yes, it's still headed for the lower Neuse River toward Minnesott."

It was about that time that Essie asked the inevitable, "Where are we in relationship to the waterspout, Cappy?"

"This is not good. We're pretty much right in the path if it continues to head down river."

The words were barely out of my mouth when the previously dark sky got as black as night. The wind started to pick up dramatically.

"Essie. Put your life jacket on and throw me mine." In seconds were both wearing our PFDs.

"What do we do now, Cappy?"

"The channel here is pretty narrow. I don't want to get thrown onto the shore. We need to get the anchor out. I'll hold us into the wind and you go drop anchor."

"Will do."

I could see the tension on her face. Essie does not frighten easily. As she made her way forward, the wind continued to build and she had to literally crawl to keep from being blown overboard. By the time she got to the bow it was blowing over sixty knots. She untied the small safety line used to secure the anchor and gave the large CQR anchor a push. It dove quickly into the dark water. Essie, after her previous anchoring scare, stayed well clear of the rode which was peeling out quickly, and she practically ran back to the cockpit. She went below and put the companionway boards in behind her. In spite of the seriousness of the situation, I had to chuckle at the obvious display of every man for themselves that was occurring at that moment. She was very scared. I looked forward to see if the anchor rode had grabbed. It was definitely a surprise to see that Essie had forgotten to tie off the end of the rope. It was peeling out at an alarming rate and would do nothing to stop us from being blown ashore. I don't know exactly how hard the wind was blowing but suffice to say it was almost hurricane strength. As I was looking at the pitch black howling sky, it started to hail, really large, cold hail and the temperature dropped like we had stepped from the desert onto the North Pole. I had to leave the wheel and go cleat off the anchor rode immediately. *Last Dance* was heeling at least thirty degrees and I knew we were going to be aground very quickly. I made my way forward on the slanted deck. The rope was shooting out so fast I had trouble grabbing it as I knew I could never hold it and it would cut my hand off if I even tried. I reached way back on the rode to the hawser where the anchor rode came from under the deck in the locker. I grabbed it as far back as I could and yanked it faster than the anchor was pulling it and threw a loop around the bow cleat. It caught instantly and the amount of tension was incredible. I ran back to the cockpit and took the wheel to attempt to keep us pointed into the wind. I couldn't judge how much line was loose in the water that had left the deck or how far the boat would go before it set. In only seconds we were starting to bounce along the bottom. I was thinking the worst. We would be blown onto shore and laid over, so far into the shallows that there would be no way to get ourselves free without calling a professional towing company to come from Beaufort and pull us out. Just as we touched bottom I saw the bow swing violently to port as the anchor rode caught. It tightened up like we had been dropped off the side of a cliff with only the rope to hold us. The set was good and solid. The position we were in seemed to be perfect. The anchor and the bottom would both be on our side to prevent the winds from pushing us any closer to shore. I never actually saw the funnel cloud. I know we were in some powerful winds and large hail. Later I would see a photograph taken from another boat in the area that clearly showed the monstrous waterspout almost exactly where we had been located as it passed. All I can gather is that we were so close to it that we couldn't see it. The photo gave me chills. The waterspout and violent weather disappeared as quickly as it came. I was smiling when Essie started to remove the boards sealing her into *Last Dance*'s cabin.

"Is it over? Are we safe?"

"Yep. We're safe. We probably wouldn't have made it if you hadn't gone forward in the height of the storm and set the anchor. Great job!" I determined to never tell her the whole story.

It's always been curious to me that as scary as events like the waterspout are when they are happening, these are the trips I remember the most as time goes by. From the tales I've heard from other sailors, I think the same is true for them. We continued on to Northwest Creek Marina and secured *Last Dance*'s new slip throughout the rest of a calm, warm afternoon.

Late in the afternoon, a Catalina 36 pulled in across from us and tied up. The name on the boat was *Soundwaves*. A couple got out and looked over our way, at the new boat on the dock. I smiled as I walked over to them.

"Hi neighbor. I'm Les and this is Susanne or Essie as I call her. We'll be here for about a month before we head south."

"I'm Tom Joseph and this is my wife Karen. We live here in New Bern and have been keeping our boat here for about five years. Look forward to getting to know you. Say, we're having a little get-together over at our house this coming Friday. Love to have you both over. It's just for drinks around 8."

"Well, I'm game if Essie is onboard."

Essie came over right behind me. "Sounds wonderful. We'll be there. Where do you live?"

"We are about four houses down from the Tryon Palace."

"You must be in a very old house."

"It is. About two hundred and fifty years to be precise. We've got a couple of ghosts and a dachshund name Homer. He is to be feared far more than ghosts. And here he comes."

The cutest little black dog you ever saw came straight over to me and offered his belly for my scratching pleasure. I accepted his gracious offer and soon we were the best of friends.

9

Over the next several days Essie and I worked like we were possessed. We could see the finish line now and we were hungry to grab the brass ring. By Wednesday night we felt like we had done all we could to get *Last Dance* ready to go. We were down to just loading provisions aboard and tossing the dock lines. We decided to anchor out in a nearby cove for the evening and have a quiet night of celebration. We shoved off about six p.m. and an hour later had the anchor down in Upper Broad Creek. I opened a bottle of red wine; Essie fixed some chips and salsa; and I dialed up our favorite romantic singer, Luis Miguel, on the stereo. We settled back to savor the moment.

"You know Cappy, we've been together almost a year."

"That's right. So much has happened that it went by as if it were only a few days."

"I know. It's been hectic and magical at the same time."

"We were so lucky to find each other."

I knew that Essie would jump on that statement. Her philosophy had always been that everything happens for a reason. You might say that everything is a part of a greater plan than we know.

"I don't believe luck had anything to do with it. Our pickers were broken so somebody a lot smarter than us put us together.

With our age difference and no friends in common, the chances of us just running into each other were zero in my book. We were supposed to find each other at this point in our lives and we did. I'm just grateful that we are here together. I can finish out my life now knowing what it's like to really be loved and in love."

"What a beautiful thought. You're right. We are very fortunate to be here together. Things have worked out the way they were supposed to all along. I want us to just stay together and enjoy every minute of the rest of our lives."

With a big smile, Essie seized the moment. "While we're on that subject there's something I feel like I need to say."

"Have at it, Miss Essie."

"I believe in marriage and not in playing house. If you feel as strongly about 'us' as I do, then I want to have a commitment. I don't want to be your perpetual date from here to eternity."

"You mean get married?"

"You are so quick. Sometimes I marvel at how in tune you are."

"Okay, Miss wiseguy. I get it. I have to say, after my last experience with marriage, it's hard to consider jumping back into it."

"You don't think for a moment that our marriage would be at all like your first marriage, do you?"

"No. But I didn't think that one would end up like it did either. I'm too old to survive going through that again."

"I've told you that I love you and that I'll be here for you for the rest of your life. You believe that?"

"With all my heart."

"Well the rest is up to you then. It's already been a year and I'm not going to wait forever. That's the last thing I'm going to say about it."

"I understand completely. I love you and I'll give this the thought it deserves over the next couple of weeks if that's okay with you."

"That's exactly what I wanted you to say. Now, what do you say we just lie back here in the cockpit and let old Luis get us in the mood?"

"I'm already in the mood. You keep me there."

By noon the next day we were back at the marina. I met Lou for lunch at a little bar next to the marina where they fixed cheeseburgers that were almost as good as those at the Royal James Cafe. Lou preferred diner food most any time. I told him about the conversation I'd had the evening before with Essie. He didn't hesitate to tell me that he thought she was the best thing that ever happened to me and if I didn't marry her, he and Stuart were going to whip my ass, in those exact words.

"I guess that makes it pretty clear. As scared as I am to try it again, I don't want to lose her. I think I'll pop the question next week. We can call our trip to the Bahamas our honeymoon. She's just so much younger than me. I really don't see what she sees in me."

"We don't either, Les. But then, it's not for us to second guess these things. Just go ahead and be thankful that she doesn't have good eyesight."

"Bastard."

"Moron."

Lou was a great guy and certainly the most "no bullshit" person I'd ever known. He loved sailboats as much as I did and the time we spent together was like being with a brother. He had started working summers with the North Carolina Ferry System as a captain of a ferry that took cars and passengers between Ocracoke Island and Hatteras Island on the Outer Banks. That meant he would be gone every other week for a seven day shift of twelve hour days. Helen stayed in New Bern in the new home they had built on Spring Creek. Lou was wealthy in his own right and didn't need to work. He just loved working on these big boats.

"Les, I've talked it over with Helen and I think we may join you on the trip to the Bahamas. We haven't been anywhere in a while, with as much as I've been working on the ferry and building the new house. I need a break and Helen loves spending time with you guys. So let's do it."

"Lou, that's great. I was hoping you would decide to come with us. It'll be fun having you guys alongside us on *Zephyr*; the fact that you've done it many times already will just make the trip that much easier. Plus, you know all the little hard-to-get to spots that most folks never see."

"I'm looking forward to it also, Les. Now, how about another burger? Helen wouldn't let me eat two of these if she were here. I love these things. They're like the ones I used to get at the drive-in burger joints when I was in high school."

We talked about the upcoming trip and planned our itinerary for another hour. Lou would work one more week on the ferry and then we'd hit the waterway south. I could barely contain myself. This is what I had been waiting for all my life. Of course, having Essie with me made it all that much better.

Friday evening we went to the Josephs for a small party to meet some of their friends and see their very old house. As we walked up to the door I noticed the historical home marker mounted on the wall beside it. It said the house was built in 1720 and rebuilt in 1840. As we entered I had to get on Tom about his fraudulent statements about how old the house was.

"Tom, what kind of scam are you pulling here?"

"What are you talking about?"

"You said the house was almost three hundred years old and now we see that it's practically new. It was all rebuilt in 1840, just a few years ago."

"I know; I'm embarrassed. I just wanted you to think the place was special. I kinda fudged I guess."

"No problem. Didn't think I'd catch that, did you?"

"Oh, you're sharp alright. Now get your sorry ass in here and meet some people."

We were introduced to several couples we hadn't met before but whom we enjoyed meeting. It looked to be an interesting evening. The phone rang and Karen excused herself. Essie and I circulated the room introducing ourselves and doing our best to associate names with faces so we wouldn't have to keep asking people what their names were. Small talk was flowing and Tom had gotten out some interesting liquors to sample. We had barely taken a sip when Karen came back into the room and walked straight over to Essie and me. She had a shocked look on her face and was absolutely pale.

"I just got a call that Lou has died. He had a heart attack just a little while ago while running the ferry in Hatteras. I'm so sorry."

I was stunned. Essie was in a state of disbelief. "Our Lou? Are you sure? Who called?"

"It was Shelia Stovall. She's over with Helen at their house. I told them you were here and Helen said to please come over."

"This is unbelievable. I'm stunned. We're going to have to leave right now. Tom, Karen, thank you for having us over. We'll come back again when this is all in the past."

"No problem, guys. I understand. Tell Helen we're very sorry for her and to just let us know if there's anything we can do."

"I will."

We drove straight from downtown New Bern to Fairfield Harbor where Helen and Lou's home was located. Northwest Creek Marina was included in Fairfield so it was only a block from our boat. I was deep in thought all the way over. Essie and I both were at a loss for words.

"I knew he was working too hard. He said last week he was tired of taking blood pressure medicine and he thought he'd stop and control it with diet and exercise. I bet he quit cold turkey."

"You know Lou. He thought it; he did it. I'm sure Helen is devastated. Lou took care of everything for her. With her kidneys in such bad shape, needing a transplant and all, he tried to make things as easy for her as he could. Whatever she needs I want to do for her."

"I'm with you, Essie. You feel her out and see what you think we can do to help her."

It was a very difficult few days for everyone who knew and loved Lou and Helen. He had friends everywhere and the calls kept coming in to Helen. The funeral service was as draining as anything I've ever been through. I think the hardest part was when Lou's son Chris, the deaf youngster Lou had adopted when he married Helen, got up to tell how he felt about his dad. There was an interpreter there who watched Chris' sign language and then spoke the words to those in attendance. Chris cried openly and made moaning sounds as he signed his message. Everyone in the chapel was tearing up and even the interpreter cried as she spoke his words.

Lou was only sixty-four years old when he died and was buried on his sixty-fifth birthday. His passing had a profound effect on me. It made me realize how fast the hands were moving on my own life clock. Whatever it was I hadn't done that I felt I needed to, I better get about doing. Lou had spent the last twenty-five years of his life doing just what he wanted to. I had never done anything but work and worry until this moment. It was time for me to take Essie and go follow our dreams. Lou's death cemented my convictions.

We helped Helen with anything we could for several weeks after the funeral. She had a lot of friends and family besides us so she was being well looked out for. We pushed back the departure date on our cruise two weeks to be there for her. The night before we were to leave, we had dinner with her at her house.

Cappy and Lou

"Les, Essie, I'm going to miss you guys. I want you to go though. Lou really wanted to go with you and I did too. That can't happen now but I would be very upset with you if you didn't do this. You take *Last Dance* and go on that trip. You never know how long you have. I've got something I want to give you."

Helen handed me a highly polished brass dinner bell with "Captain" inscribed on it.

"Lou's daughter Audra had this inscribed as a birthday gift for Lou. I want you to take it on the trip with you and every time you get ready to eat you can ring the bell and think of Lou. It'll be like he's there with you."

"We will, Helen. And don't worry about Lou being with us. He'll always be with us. And we'll call back and check on you as much as we can."

"Don't worry about me. Shelia is here with me and will be for the next several months. You go and see the Bahamas. When you get back, I want to see your pictures and hear all about what you did."

"You can count on it."

We stayed until about eleven p.m. but finally had to leave. Sunrise would come early and we wanted to put in a full day heading south.

10

Light began leaking through the curtains in the aft cabin very early. The trauma we had been through with Lou's death had taken more of a toll on us than we thought. Events that are emotionally draining can sometimes be more exhausting than physical labor. We were both tired but we were excited so we forced ourselves to get out of a soft comfortable bed. Always positive, Essie came over and gave me a huge hug and a kiss on the forehead.

"Cappy, take care of the morning breath and I'll move that kiss a little closer to your lips. Want some coffee?"

"I thought you'd never ask. Make it a full mug. I'm tired, but I'm anxious to get going."

Essie fixed us both a cup and no sooner had we sat down at the salon table to sip it and bite on a granola bar than we heard voices on our finger pier.

"Ahoy, *Last Dance*! Time to rise and shine. Permission to come aboard and borrow a cup of coffee."

The voices were unmistakable. I stepped out into the cockpit and there on the dock was Jim, Sara, David, Leigh, Tom, and Karen.

"We've come to see you off. Kinda surprised to see us, aren't you?"

"To tell you the truth, in a word, yes!"

"We weren't about to let you guys sneak outta here without seeing you off. How far do you think you're going to get today?"

"Probably just to Taylor Creek in Beaufort. We'll anchor out tonight and get one more full night's sleep under our belts and tomorrow, if the weather's good, we want to go offshore all the way to Lake Worth."

"Not going down the ditch, eh?"

"Nope. We did that on *Calypso*. It's fun but slow and we're anxious to see palm trees and clear water."

"Don't blame you. I wish we were going with you. Hey, maybe next trip."

"I certainly hope so. I'll call whenever we're within distance of a cell tower so that our phone will work and let you know where we are."

"Please. We want to hear about all the fun you're having while we stay behind and work."

"Jim, I notice you're not saying that."

"No. I'm thrilled to be working. Still on the payroll of "Days of Thunder" with Tom Cruise and Robert Duval. Having a great time. But when we're wrapped, I'm taking *The Lone Ranger* and heading south myself. I want to be at least to Florida before summer's over. Maybe we'll see you there."

"That would be great. Well, as much as I'd like to stay and chew the fat with you, we've got to get underway. You fellas want to help me with the dock lines and electric cable?"

"Love to."

Within minutes all our lines were loose and on deck. We hugged everyone and said our final farewells. I pushed the lever into reverse and we backed out of the slip. It seemed only a short while ago that we were doing the same on *Calypso* as Essie and I and, oh yes, John Silver a/k/a Bob Leisey headed out. I certainly hoped this would be a little less stressful adventure.

Just before we did a 180 degree turn and headed away, we waved to our friends back on the dock. That was always a nostalgic moment. You never know when you tell someone you'll see them later if that's truly going to be the case. After Lou's passing, that was clearer to me than ever before. In just moments the marina was a small silhouette on shore. We were on our way once more. *Last Dance* was going to be a lot more comfortable home afloat than *Calypso*. She had a walk-through to the aft cabin that *Calypso* didn't and a lot more room in general. Her hull was longer and heavier and her ride was a lot smoother. I wouldn't put *Calypso* down as she took us through a lot, but I felt good about moving up to *Last Dance*.

The day was warm and calm. Being a weekday there were almost no other sailboats on the way to Beaufort. The few we passed were snowbirds in Adam's Creek headed north for the summer. We were certainly going against the grain to head south this time of year. I suppose we should have been concerned with hurricanes but I determined that if I waited until after the season it would be November and we might not have the time or money to go. We'd seize the moment while we had it.

We arrived in Beaufort at 4:30 in the afternoon and didn't worry about even going to shore. We had a lot of supplies on board and were self-sufficient. We'd turn in early and try to be in the ocean when the sun came up. I opened up a Corona and Essie got her usual small glass of wine and we sat up in the cockpit watching the sun go down. I turned on the VHF weather channel to get a last minute update. The forecast looked good. Actually, it looked very good for offshore. Light easterly winds, eight to twelve knots, with seas under two feet. No change was forecast for the next two days. Traveling night and day, we would be almost to Florida by then. It couldn't have been a better weather window.

We almost fell asleep in the cockpit. I was resting on the bulkhead at the back of the cockpit seat and Essie was lying between my legs with her back on top of my chest. She felt like she was custom made to be next to me. By 8:00 we slipped down to the aft cabin and tucked in for the night.

By 4 a.m. we were both wide awake. Adrenalin always serves as an alarm clock for me when I'm getting ready to go sailing, especially so if it's going to be offshore. We checked the engine oil and water, fired up the old diesel, and weighed anchor in less than thirty minutes. It was a warm morning so shorts were the order of the day from the moment we got underway. It took another half hour to get past the last spit of land on Beaufort Inlet. Fort Macon, the pre-Civil War outpost, loomed large to our starboard as did the Coast Guard facility based there. Off to our port we could just make out Cape Lookout lighthouse and its periodic beacon that warned mariners of the danger of Diamond Shoals.

We stayed in the ship channel until we reached the number one marker and then set our course on a southeasterly direction to ease offshore a ways. With the wind slightly out of the northeast it was a tight reach and we only headed east enough to make some distance away from shore. The wind was light as predicted. We decided to motor sail to maintain some speed. The wind alone could only help us muster three to four knots and with the motor basically idling at 1400 RPMs we easily maintained seven.

The seas were calm and overall it was a perfect day to be offshore. We were visited during the day by dolphins who played in our bow wave a while, disappeared, only to return an hour later and join us for another short period. Essie reveled in their beauty and playfulness.

"If there is such a thing as reincarnation, I want to come back as a porpoise. All they do is play, eat, and make baby porpoises. How could life be any better than that?"

"I'm with you on that. They must be in some sort of heaven for achievements in a previous life. We should be that lucky. If they check my record closely, I'll probably be sent back as a catfish."

"Why a catfish?"

"They live in very muddy water, eat poop from everything else that lives there, and have whiskers as long as their body. And, of course, if they get caught by a fisherman, they get skinned and peeled. Yep, that would be my fate."

"I don't agree with that at all. I think you'd come back as a sailfish. You'd be handsome, have your own sail, and be able to travel the oceans of the world for your entire life."

"Okay, I'd go for that. Beautiful out here, isn't it?"

"I always like it when we are out of sight of land. The ocean is so immense it just makes everything else seem insignificant by comparison. It's constantly in motion and it's like it's all alive, a huge beautiful creature that owns most of the planet."

"Very good visual. It can also be a very nasty owner when it makes up its mind to be. We've both seen it when it was in that mood."

"Yes. That ride into Charleston last year. I'll always remember that one wave. It must have been fifty feet tall."

"I can still feel us rising up as it went under us. Makes the hair on my arms stand up. But it's calm today and we're making great time. Bahamas here we come."

We couldn't have asked for a more perfect day. The next morning, a Wednesday, brought more of the same. We were now approaching the latitude that ran through Georgia and were on target for a quick trip south. We slept in shifts so we could stay awake through the night and keep a lookout for large ships making their way up and down the coast. We were in their waters and needed to watch for them closely. As large as they were they still managed to crank out speeds of twenty to twenty-five knots. That's respectable speed for a small speedboat. It also meant they could go from being completely out of sight to running you over in less than fifteen minutes. Falling asleep on watch could be fatal. Essie and I both understood that clearly and if we ever felt sleepy, we'd wake the other up and break the normal on and off routine we had established. Safety would always be our first consideration.

There was no moon out this evening. It was still fairly calm with a freshening breeze. We were moving along nicely without the engine at about six knots. It's always a little unnerving to be moving through the water with almost no visibility. In reality, there's very little to hit other than another boat. There is the remote danger of cargo containers that have fallen off a ship and are floating just beneath the surface. To strike one at four knots or over would certainly rip a hole in the hull and mean you were going down. At night, especially a dark night, those sorts of thoughts can't help but run through a skipper's mind. I knew that the greater danger was being run over by a ship, so we always kept a sharp lookout for lights on the horizon. This particular night, as dark as it was, would actually make a small light in the distance stand out. About three a.m., I was on watch when I saw another ship's light in the distance. I figured it would turn away in a while as most others did. It didn't happen. It became brighter and clearer. Before long it was easy to see that it was a combination red and green bow light as would be found on a boat more the size of ours than a ship. It was bouncing up and down, also indicating a smaller boat. Before long I could actually hear the motor running. It was deep and throaty, meaning a strong inboard. We were over forty miles offshore and to find a smaller powerboat out here would be rare. I was very dubious. It continued to head straight toward us.

"Essie, Essie. Do you hear me?"

I could hear her stirring below as she struggled to pull on some pants for her watch. She wasn't aware that her watch wouldn't come on for another hour. She came up to the top of the companionway steps still rubbing the sleep from her eyes. "Is it four already? Feels like I just laid down."

"No. We've got company out here. I wouldn't wake you but this is pretty unusual."

"I see them. It's a small boat with a combination bow light."

"Yeah, seeing a small powerboat this far out at night is strange."

"Think they're fishing? Maybe they're here getting ready for sunup to drag a bait for marlin."

"They're heading straight for us. That's what bothers me."

"You think they're up to no good?"

"It's possible. Go get my pistol and let's put it under the seat cushion just in case."

"I'm on it."

By the time Essie came back up with the gun, the boat was only a hundred yards off. I could hear the motor slowing down. They wanted to come alongside us. I had a very bad feeling about this.

I could see as the boat came alongside us that it was going to be worse than I even thought. The boat held a crew that looked more like a New York street gang than sailors. They were dark and bearded with an almost foreign look, maybe from South America. The boat had no name or identifying numbers. It was about fifty feet long and looked like an offshore sport fisherman modified to be a gunboat. Some of the men yelled to each other in Spanish and threw out fenders on the port side of their boat. They came up close and I could plainly see they were all holding automatic weapons. I couldn't believe that pirates would be operating in these waters. Besides, getting a ransom for us or any money for this old boat would be close to a joke. Another thought came to me. Drugs. They wanted our boat to run drugs.

In moments they secured lines to our boat and came aboard. Their apparent leader came over to me in the cockpit. He spoke very broken English.

"Good evening, Captain. Your name and mine are not important. I'll make this very quick so as not to worry your lady any more than necessary. We don't want to kill you. It's not necessary for what we are about. We are going to take your boat and use it for two days. After that time we will take it offshore and sink it. You will collect your insurance, buy a new boat and be better off for your troubles."

"I guess that could work if I had any insurance which I don't. And what happens to us when you take our boat?"

"Your dinghy looks to be seaworthy. The weather is calm. You will start rowing toward land. Someone will find you, I'm sure. We'll of course leave you some water, food, and a light. After all, we're business men, not animals. That's enough talk."

He motioned to his men to lower the dinghy. They moved very quickly and appeared to know exactly what needed to be done. This was not their first adventure of this sort. One of the thugs went below with Essie and directed her to fill a pillowcase with any supplies she thought we'd need. I sat down in the cockpit with a gun barrel pointed at me. Just as she came back up the companionway I took a calculated gamble and slid our gun out from under my cushion. I reached for Essie's bag and when she handed it to me I opened the top up as if looking to see what supplies she had gathered. As I closed it back up I looked over toward the drug boat and the guard followed my glance. I then dropped the pistol into the bag. Our dinghy was pulled alongside and we were practically pushed into it. One of the men untied the line to the dinghy and threw it in with us. We quickly drifted away from our only home. I looked over at Essie who was staring at them. She had no tears in her eyes as many women would certainly have running down their cheeks in such a situation. Not my Essie.

"Bastards. They will live to regret doing this. If it's the last thing I do I'll get them for this. They just made the biggest mistake they're ever going to make." She paused, leaned back against the hull of the inflatable dinghy and yelled at the top of her lungs. "You sorry bastards. You rotten creeps. I will get even with you."

I had never seen her this mad. Not upset, mad. Really mad. They didn't let us take the dinghy motor, just the oars, some food and water. We could ration what we had and go several days, maybe more. My biggest concern was the freshening weather. I didn't want to be forty miles at sea in a nine foot long inflatable dinghy.

"Well, we better start coming up with a plan, Essie. Just sitting out here waiting for help isn't going to cut it. Here's my thought. The wind is still out of the east. We can take the pillow case and an oar and jury-rig a sail. We can at least be moving toward the coast."

"Let's get on it."

We ripped the pillow case and moved the food into a small locker under the dinghy seat. I took the shoelaces from my tennis shoes and lashed the pillowcase to one of the two aluminum oars. I took off my belt and lashed the oar to the seat. Essie's bra straps became the lines we needed to control tension on the bottom of the makeshift sail.

"We're not moving fast but we're moving. I'll take the first shift and you try to sleep. The less moving around, the better. Everything we do takes energy and we're going to need all of it to survive this. We may not be found for days, if at all. We'll conserve the water, food, and ourselves."

I had read every book I could get my hands on about sailing over the years. I'd read numerous accounts of survival at sea by people in similar situations to where we were. Some of their actions came to mind and at least gave us a plan of attack. We would not go down without a fight.

I couldn't go to sleep the entire night. I was very concerned about how long we would be out here and also on high alert for any ships that might be headed our way. On one hand, it would be great to see a ship so we could get rescued and out of this dinghy but, on the other, we could also be run over and a huge ship wouldn't even know they did it. The wind picked up all night. Essie tossed and turned trying to get comfortable without much success. If she hadn't been so exhausted, I doubt she would have slept ten minutes.

"Hey, Cappy. See any boats? I'm sorry I wasn't much help through the night."

"Haven't seen anything. The wind is picking up but at least it's still out of the east and pushing us toward the coast. The dinghy seems to be holding air. If we move at just two knots and the wind direction remains out of the east, we should be getting within sight of land by tomorrow."

"Thank God they let us have food and water. This would be a lot more difficult if we were starving."

"Amen."

For the next four hours the wind continued to build and the waves followed suit. There were now swells around six feet high everywhere and a little bit of white on their tops. The sky was darkening and I was getting very apprehensive of what was going to happen through the afternoon. I watched the waves rise and fall around us and couldn't help but notice something moving just under their surface. There seemed to be an occasional shadow that looked like a log about a foot or so deep in the waves.

"Oh, my God, Cappy! I saw a shark right over there."

"I know. I didn't want to tell you but there are several and they seem to be following our shadow."

"What else can happen? All we need now is for a submarine to surface underneath us. I'm really scared of sharks."

"I don't like them either."

I didn't want to mention to Essie what I was thinking. This reminded me of what happened to the crew of *Trashman*. It was a fifty-four foot Alden that sank off the coast of North Carolina about this same distance out. There were five on board a small dinghy. Two of the guys on board drank salt water and became delirious. They jumped in thinking they could swim to shore. Sharks circling their dinghy ate them both in only seconds. There were dozens of them following their boat. Two of the crew were eventually picked up after five or six days of drifting. The rest died. Two were killed by sharks and one died due to a diabetic coma. We had fresh water on board so there was no chance of us drinking salt water. I wasn't about to even stick a hand in the water. Twice that evening we felt very strong bumps against the bottom of our little boat. It was getting very scary. To top it all off, the waves were now large enough that we were sliding down the face of them.

"I hate to do it but I've got to take down our sail. Let's stow it under the seat in the locker. We don't need anything to make us less stable in these waves. There's enough wind that we'll still be moving toward shore."

"Do whatever you think we need to do to live through this, Cappy. I'd hate to think that after all we've been through that we would die out here like this."

"We're not going to die, Essie."

"What makes you so sure of that?"

"Because if we die, you won't be able to attend your own wedding."

"What wedding?"

"The one we're going to have when we get back to New Bern."

"Is this a proposal?"

"If you'll have me. I know I'm not much of a catch, but I love you more than anything and I'll be good to you 'til my last day."

"I had hoped for a little more romantic setting than this. But I've thought it over and, mister, you've got yourself a wife. Yes, I want to marry you with all my heart. And even if you're out of your head out here and not knowing what you're doing or saying, I'm going to hold you to it."

"I know exactly what I'm doing."

There, miles at sea, adrift in a tiny rubber spec, we embraced and even though all around us there was danger and great risk, I felt as secure as I ever had. I would do everything in my power to get us home. The wind and sea built and by sundown we were in a gale. The seas were large, the wind was blowing a steady thirty knots and we might as well have been on a water ride at Disney World. If conditions got any worse we would be in trouble. Having the dinghy flip and toss us into these unfriendly waters would be a dangerous turn of events. As it got darker, we could no longer see the large shapes that had been with us for hours. We both knew sharks fed at night and we didn't want to be on their menu.

"Cappy, I'm getting very scared. I just don't think we can keep this thing upright all night. I'm so tired I can barely think straight."

Lightning flashed at that moment and indicated that the storm was now on top of us and might get even worse.

"This is good, Essie. Thunderstorms don't usually last very long. The wind picks up and after a while they move away."

"I'm afraid it might last longer than I do."

Several strong lightning blasts lit up the sky like a fireworks display on the Fourth of July. The third flash made a wave top translucent and again, there was the large shadow just under the surface. They hadn't forgotten about us. They were probably licking their chops just waiting for the dink to flip us into their world. I was already wet and cold but this sight sent chills down the back of my neck. I didn't see how the situation could get much worse. The heart of the storm bore down on us more fiercely than before. The wind was so loud it hid the sounds of the waves crashing. The dinghy started to slide down a monstrous wave. We were in the middle trying to stay low but the angle of the wave dumped us both to the low side. That lifted the trailing edge of the dinghy and the wind picked it up like a cheap kite. It flipped over on top of us and, that quickly, we were both in the water. The water was actually warmer than the air. My immediate thought was to not get separated from Essie or the dinghy. I yelled as loudly as I could to be heard over the storm.

"Essie, grab a dinghy handle on the outside of the hull."

There were four rubber handles on the hulls that were used to carry the dink. There were two on each side, one fore and one aft. I saw Essie grab it and I reached up for the other.

"We've got to flip it back over and not let go of it."

"Let's do it quick. We're not alone here."

"Count of three, push the handle up as hard as you can. I'll do the same."

The dinghy only weighed about seventy pounds. All we had to do was get the side up slightly and the same wind that flipped it over would hit it again, hopefully righting it.

"One, two, three, push!"

We both gave it all we had. The side went up and then fell down back on top of us.

"Try again. One two three."

Again we failed to get enough air under the hull.

"Cappy, I'm too tired to do it again. I can't lift it anymore."

"Essie, if you're going to marry me, you're going to have to do this. Again, one, two, three."

I gave it everything I had. I could see the strain and fear on Essie's face. The dink lifted up and this time the wind caught it, flipping it like a matchbox.

"It's over. Get back in."

"I can't, Cappy. I don't have the strength."

I moved over to her, grabbed the side of the small handle she was holding. "Essie, climb up on my back and shoulders. I'll drop down in the water as far as I can. Please hurry. Do it now."

I dropped down under the surface as far as I could and still hold the handle. Essie pulled up to where her knees were on my back and then my shoulders. I felt her lift up and then go over my head. She was back onboard. I also felt something that jarred me more than just about anything I'd ever felt in my life. A large abrasive bump on the side of my right leg was unmistakable. I knew exactly what it was and what it meant. Sharks will normally test their victims by bumping them before they attack. I was not going to wait for the second run at me.

"Essie, grab my hand and help me up. I'll pull up as hard as I can with the handle too."

I gave it every ounce of strength I had and Essie pulled at the same time. I just barely made it up on the side of the inflatable tube. I then rolled into the floor of the boat beside Essie. I looked back at the water and saw a very large fin brush alongside the dinghy exactly where I had been holding it. The now familiar chill revisited my spine.

"Thanks, Essie. That was the last of what I had. We need to stay flat on the bottom of the dink. Stay spread out to distribute our weight. We can't risk falling to one side again."

"I'll try. Your leg is bleeding. It looks like you fell on a gravel driveway."

"My leg was 'sanded' by one of our friends swimming under us."

"Oh, my God! You're kidding, right?"

"Nope. One of them was sizing me up for dinner."

"Don't even tell me anything else about it."

We lay on the bottom of the dink for the next two hours. We were bounced from underneath more than once. I'm sure our friends below us knew there was a good sized meal just on the other side of this small piece of rubber. Several times over the next hour the wind tried its best to lift the dink but our plan worked and we stayed right-side up. The winds abated during the night.

Dawn came up bright and warm. The ocean was almost glassy with no waves. With no waves and a bright sun shining deep into the clear ocean water, we could plainly see at least twenty large sharks, anywhere from six to ten foot long slowly moving around our little raft. My gaze drifted up from the water's surface and for just a minute I felt like I must have grit in my eyes. I rubbed them and stared again. There, just on the horizon to our west, a water tower was plainly visible.

"Essie, look. We're within striking distance of shore. We can't be more than five or six miles out."

"How can you tell?"

"Look right over there." I pointed toward the spot on shore.

"Is that a building?"

"No. It's a water tower. It's right over the horizon. We should be seeing some fishing boats on a nice day like this. God only knows there's plenty of fish around here."

"If we get out of this, it will be a miracle. To have the wind blow for two full days toward shore was too much to hope for. How will we get a boat's attention?"

"The pistol is in the locker still, isn't it? If a boat gets close enough to hear, I'll fire a shot in the air to get their attention."

We didn't have to wait long. We heard it before we saw it. The loud drone of large diesels pushing a sport fisherman drew our view to a distant spec on the water. It was pushing up a large bow wave and headed somewhat in our direction. I got the gun out of the small locker beneath the dinghy seat. The boat's course looked like it would bring it to within a half mile of our position. I waited until I felt it was as close as it would get before moving away. I fired a shot into the air. We both waited to see the boat turn toward us. It didn't happen. It never slowed, turned, or acknowledged that they saw or heard us.

"What's wrong, Cappy? Why didn't they stop?"

"They probably can't hear anything as loud as the engines are and as strong as they have them turned up. We have five more bullets. There'll be others. Keep your eyes open. I almost hated to tell Essie what I noticed: The wind was building again, this time from the wrong direction. It was pushing us away from shore. I could see smoke on shore where someone was either burning off a field or debris. Within an hour, the water tower could no longer be seen. At least four boats had come within our line of sight over the morning but none close enough for us to attract their attention. We had two bullets left and they had to work or we would be in an even more dire situation very quickly. We were starting to run out of drinking water and we were both getting very red from the sun. I could hear desperation in Essie's voice. She was trying to be strong and God knows she is a strong woman. There's only so much anyone can deal with and we were close to our limit.

We stayed low in the dinghy as the wind started to fill in. I was not looking forward to another night of trying to keep the dink upright and not feed the fish. We had both gotten very quiet and into our thoughts. I kept thinking this would be so ironic to find someone I wanted to spend the rest of my life with, somebody who loved me in return, and especially someone who shared my ridiculous dreams, and yet here we were. Probably not going to be around to live out those dreams. My kids would never know what happened to me. I realized that I didn't know anything about Essie's family. Those were questions I would ask if we somehow made it through this.

"Cappy, what is that over there?"

"Where?"

"Over there, just to the right. Is that smoke?"

"No. That's a sail. It's headed in our direction. Let's wait 'til they are the closest they're going to be and I'll fire both shots. They're sailing, not motoring. They'll be able to hear the shots."

It seemed like two hours, but in reality it was only ten minutes at the most when the small sloop reached its closest position to us.

I said a prayer and stood up in the dinghy. I pulled the trigger and then started to wave. The boat maintained its course. I got Essie to stand up with me and fired the last shot. Essie waved the pillowcase sail as hard as she could. The sloop tacked over hard and started to point straight at us. Had they heard? Did they see us? When they got within a hundred yards we started to scream. A young man moved to the bow of the boat and yelled back to us. "We see you. We see you. Sit down. Don't fall in."

The sight of that boat coming toward us was the single best thing I'd experienced since the first time Essie and I shared a bed. Adrenalin was running through our bodies and we had a burst of energy I didn't think was possible. The sailboat came alongside of us and while I held the dinghy tight up against it, Essie jumped aboard. I followed her immediately.

"Do you want us to tow the dinghy in?"

"Well, it saved us so I guess we should save it if we can."

"No problem. I'll tie a line to the bow. I'm Jim Singer and that's my wife Vanessa on the wheel. How long have you guys been out here?"

"Our boat was stolen two days ago by drug dealers. They said they weren't killers and did us the huge favor of setting us adrift in the ocean about forty miles out. I really didn't think we were going to make it. We owe you big time."

"You don't owe us a thing. Geez, would you look at all the sharks out here. What's that all about?"

"You just stole their lunch. They've been following us for two days."

"Thank God we came out here today. We almost didn't come. What do you want us to do?"

"First, let's call the Coast Guard and get them looking for our boat."

Jim and Vanessa Singer – Saved us from the sharks

"We've got a VHF radio right by the companionway. You want to do the honors?"

"Thank you. Thank you so much. Do you have some water?"

"Water, beer, wine, soft drinks, whatever you want."

"I'd love some water. I know Essie needs some. By the way, I'm Les, and she's Essie."

"Nice to meet you both."

"Again, we owe you man."

I took a huge drink from the water bottle, almost draining it in one breath. I sat down on the cockpit seat and took the radio mike. "U.S. Coast Guard, U.S. Coast Guard. *Last Dance* calling."

"Go ahead *Last Dance*. What's the nature of your problem?"

"We've had our boat stolen by drug runners and have been adrift in a dinghy for two days. We've been picked up by a sailboat and need assistance."

The conversation went on for ten minutes as we gave them every scrap of information about ourselves, our lives, and our boat. Finally, the Coast Guard radio operator announced they were sending a cutter out to meet us and take us to shore. Jim and Vanessa treated us like family for the next hour until the cutter showed up. They pulled alongside and we transferred to the Coast Guard forty-four footer for the ride back to their station. We had nowhere else to go for the moment. We had no car, no money, no identification. We hugged Jim and Vanessa and thanked them profusely. They were gracious and Jim gave us their phone number on a slip of paper. We certainly wanted to thank them properly when everything settled down.

11

The ride in on the cutter took almost an hour. The officers and crew running the boat looked like college kids they were so young. They were all very friendly, courteous, polite, but professional. The cutter captain looked to be about twenty-eight or so and took great interest in our story. When we asked about the chances of getting our boat back, he said we'd need to address that with the station commander.

"Where are we? What station are we headed to?"

"We are out of the Brunswick station. Our station Commander, Tom Pollard, will debrief you on this ordeal and help you figure out what can be done to help you."

Essie and I continued to rehydrate and rest in the cabin of the cutter. It was not a vessel designed for comfort. Everything on it was all business and at the speed we were running it was hard to relax. When we arrived at the station, Commander Pollard greeted us warmly and directed us to a rest area where we could shower and get some clean clothes on, which were Coast Guard jump suits. Nonetheless, they were greatly appreciated and feeling the hot water pour over our very fatigued bodies was almost spiritual. A young man from the station ran out to a local Subway and brought us back a large sandwich each and we ate like starved wolves. After another hour of decompressing, Commander Pollard came with a young administrative assistant to talk with us about what had transpired.

I related every detail of our ordeal that I could remember and Essie filled in any holes in my memory. I finally had to ask the question that was foremost in our thoughts. "Commander, what are the chances of getting our boat back? Will you send out a chopper or a search team to help locate it?"

"Mr. Pendleton, I know you don't want to hear this, but the best we can do is put out a notice to mariners and alert all the marinas on the East Coast to be on alert for your boat. The sheer size of the ocean and the lead time they have makes it virtually impossible to mount a search effort. You're safe and that is our primary mission. We'll help you with an insurance claim so you can get another boat."

"That's a problem. We didn't have insurance. And it was not only our boat but our only home."

"I'm truly sorry, folks. I know that's not very comforting but our hands are tied. We have to keep our choppers and cutters on the ready for people who are in danger, as you were. We can't use our assets for that type of search and we aren't authorized to look for property. If you have any idea where they were headed with your boat, which port, we could take action then."

"There's really no way to know. We appreciate your position and are thankful for you bringing us in. I'm most concerned about them saying that when they were done with our boat they were going to sink it. Whatever can be done, if anything, has to be done in a hurry or I'm afraid it will just be too little too late. We need some time to talk about what we want to do and then, if you have a phone we could use to make a few calls we might be able to get a friend to come pick us up."

"Not a problem. Follow me."

Commander Pollard led us down the hall to a small room with a table, a few vending machines, and a phone. It was obviously the break room his staff used. We thanked him again and Essie and I started to discuss our situation.

"First, Cappy, I need a huge hug. I am so thankful and relieved that we made it. Several times I thought that might be the end."

"I know, baby. I was right there with you. I don't believe we could get much closer to the next life than where we have just come from."

We embraced for a full minute. Essie shed several tears, which I'd never seen her do before. I could feel the relief flowing out of our bodies. We sat together on the hard vinyl covered bench and started to develop some sort of action plan to at least get us home, which was the first order of business and, second, to try to come up with a way to get our boat back.

"Cappy, let's call David and Leigh and see if they'll drive down. They're retired. Maybe we can offer to pay for the gas and hotel."

"I'm sure they will. I need to call the bank and get a new debit card. I'll cancel the old card number at the same time. We've still got some money in the bank. Once again, it's our cruising kitty that we'll be blowing to survive the latest disaster. Sometimes I think I'm not destined to do this dream of mine."

"Don't even talk like that. How much do you think it would cost to get a small plane and a pilot to fly us over all the marinas on the coast and see if we can spot *Last Dance* before they take her back out to sea and sink her? I don't care if she smells like marijuana or is full of spilled narcotics, I want her back. And I'd like to see all those thugs dropped at sea in a little rubber dinghy."

"Me too. That's probably too much to hope for but I agree completely with you. I think it would cost a lot of money to rent a plane and a pilot. It would probably take all our savings."

"I don't care. Do we know anyone with a plane?"

"Not that I can think of. None of our friends have that kind of money."

It was at just that moment that the same person came to mind for both us simultaneously. We said it out loud at the exact same moment.

"Vinny!"

"Cappy, you remember what he said. If there was ever anything he could do to help us we could call and count on him. I don't think we'll ever be more in need than right now."

"I wonder how we can get up with him! I had his number in my wallet and that's gone."

"Let's call Grimshaw. He got his number too. Call David and Leigh and tell them to get the number from Jim immediately and we'll give Vinny a call."

David and Leigh were almost in a state of shock by the time our call was over. They offered to do anything and everything to help us and it made us feel so much better just to hear their familiar voices on the phone. They said they'd contact Jim and get right back with us. They would also be in the car within the hour to come get us if we needed them to. You can't ask for better friends than that. Five minutes later the phone rang and Grimshaw gave us Vinny's number. He, of course, said he wanted the film rights to the story which we assured him would go to no one else. We had no clue what Vinny's response would be to such a bizarre situation, but we were at the end of our resources and willing to give it a shot.

"Hello, you got Vinny. Who is this?"

"Vinny, this is Les Pendleton. You remember Essie and me from picking you up on our boat the night you went swimming?"

"Cappy! How the hell could I ever forget you? How are you and Essie doing?"

"Vinny, we're in a situation right now and need help. You were the only person we could think of who might be able to help us."

In a conversation that sounded like it was straight out of "The Godfather," Vinny responded, "Les, Cappy, you did the right thing. Vinny never, never forgets a favor. I offered you my assistance in any way if you ever needed help and I'm ecstatic that you have called me. It is an honor and a privilege to help such wonderful people as you and Miss Essie. Now, what is the problem?"

I told Vinny in great detail what had occurred. He occasionally interjected a very expressive, "Those bastards," which let me know he was taking in every detail. He seemed to know a lot of the story and how it went without me even telling him, almost as if he had heard it before. He finally took a minute, gathered his thoughts and gave us the answer we had hoped to hear.

"Okay, Cappy, Essie. Here's what's gonna happen. I'm going to the boss, my good friend and cousin, Frank. That's Frank Albertini. He's kind of a big deal up here. The plane that picked me up in New Bern belongs to him. It's fast; he's got a great pilot; and Frank, well he's not a guy to trifle with if you get my drift. You and Essie just stay where you are and I'll have you picked up and driven over to the airport to meet me. We'll have a plan together by that time on how to approach this. Frank is really, really good at handling things like this. That's why he's the boss. I'll be down there in no more than four hours. Let them know at the Coast Guard Station that you've got a car coming to pick you up. And Cappy…"

"Yeah, Vinny."

"You tell Miss Essie not to worry about a thing. We can handle this sort of thing."

"I will, Vinny, and thanks."

"Not a problem, my friend."

We called David and Leigh and told them not to do the drive to pick us up, there was someone else already on the way. Then Essie and I dozed off in the break room for about two hours. We were tired beyond imagination. It helped to get a couple hours of actual sleep unlike being in the dinghy where we felt like sandwiches sitting on a lunch counter waiting for the waitress to take us to a table to be devoured. We were awakened by a young Coastie.

"Mr. Pendleton, there's someone here to pick you up. The car is waiting in the parking lot."

"Thank you. Please give our regards to Commander Pollard and a thank you to all the staff here for coming to get us and trying to make us comfortable."

"I will, sir. Sorry we weren't able to help you find your boat."

"I understand your situation. Perhaps we'll find it anyway."

"Yes, sir. I sure hope so."

We walked out to the parking lot where a black Mercedes 500 was waiting for us. A huge, Italian looking guy named Jimmy greeted us and opened the back door.

"Greetings from Vinny. I'm supposed to take you guys to the airport. Need to stop for anything on the way? We've still got a couple of hours before they arrive."

"They?"

"Oh yeah. Vinny's bringing a few associates of his with him that have a little more experience in these things than he does."

"What type of experience is that?"

"Oh, ex-military guys, counter-intelligence types. As luck would have it, Mr. Albertini has a few of them on the payroll that Vinny thought would be a big help in this little scenario. You'll like 'em. Very serious people."

"We are so grateful."

"Not a problem. You do something for one of our guys and they feel terrible if they can't repay the favor. They live for this sort of stuff."

"I wonder if it would be possible for you to run us by a bank so I can get some cash and then to somewhere we can get some more comfortable clothes to wear. I appreciate the Coast Guard lending us these jump suits but I'd prefer something in my size and I know Essie here would like some clothes that weren't unisex."

"You're the boss. Just tell me the name of the bank and we're on our way."

Two hours later, in new clothes and with a couple of hundred dollars in a new wallet, we waited in the general aviation terminal of the small Brunswick airport. At four hours on the dot the sleek black private jet that Vinny had boarded in New Bern appeared on approach. Essie and I walked out on the tarmac to greet them. The door opened and the steps lowered. The large guy we had met in New Bern the first time we put Vinny on the plane came out, walked straight over to us smiling.

"Les, Essie, how the heck are you guys?"

"Tank. Good to see you. To be honest, we never thought we'd see any of you again after Vinny went home. Funny how things work, isn't it?"

"You can't predict the future, my friends."

A very familiar voice came through the door to the plane. "Ah, Cappy, Essie, my great friends. Sorry you have had a problem."

Vinny walked down the steps and bypassed a handshake going immediately for a large hug from Essie and then me.

"I don't believe I've ever known anybody that had more trouble hanging on to a boat than you guys. But don't fret. Vinny is here and me and the boys are going to get her back for you."

Three more men exited the plane. Two were dressed in slacks with black polished shoes and tight fitting polo shirts. Behind them, an older gentleman wearing very expensive Guccis, tailored slacks, and a white pressed silk shirt smiled as he walked over to us. He was polished with thick white hair and a great smile. He extended his tanned arm with it's exquisite Rolex Presidential catching the sun and warmly shook my hand.

"You must be Les and this is your lady friend Essie, am I correct?"

"That's right. Thank you for coming to help us. You are?"

Vinny jumped right in with the answer and introduction. "Les, Essie, this is the boss, Frank Albertini. I've worked for him all my life. You will find no better friend than Mr. Albertini."

"You can call me Frank. Vinny has updated me a little on your problem. Why don't we go to the hotel and discuss where we are in this situation so we can develop a strategy."

"We're not in a hotel. We actually picked up some clothes at the store and came straight over here. We don't have a room."

"You do now. We'll all stay at a nice place downtown on the waterfront that Vinny arranged. Some friends of ours run it and want us to have gratis rooms there. You don't mind that I took the liberty of accepting on your behalf do you?"

"We would be thrilled to stay there. We were wondering where we would stay tonight. Our boat was our home."

"I understood that. Let's head to the hotel and have some food brought in while we work this out. I'm sure you're hungry. Am I right?"

"Yes, sir. We're right behind you."

Jimmy directed a second black Mercedes over to the terminal where two pilots, Tank, Vinny, and the others were waiting. Vinny, Frank, Essie and I got in one car and the rest followed in the other. With two black Mercedes parading downtown we must have looked like delegates to the United Nations. As we pulled into the hotel, the manager and several uniformed staff greeted us at the door. Since they were already waiting under the covered valet area when we arrived, I had to guess that they must have been determined to be standing there when we arrived no matter how long that took. I wasn't sure just how Vinny and Frank played into all of what was going on, but it was pretty obvious they were heavy hitters of some sort. People everywhere seemed anxious to do anything they could to help them. Vinny and Frank always seemed overly pleased with the special attention and never failed to acknowledge to those offering it how much it was appreciated. We were escorted to the top floor of a spectacular hotel. The concierge sent bellhops with us to open the rooms, carry luggage, and make certain we were pleased with the accommodations. Since it was the nicest hotel suite in the most expensive hotel I'd ever seen, what was there to not be pleased about? We both freshened up a little and then Vinny came in to take us to Frank's room down the hall. I thought our room was nice. Frank's looked like a luxury suite in the Bellagio in Vegas.

It was ornate, furnished with everything from a wet bar to a grand piano. Frank was sitting on the couch talking with one of his pilots.

"Les, Essie, come on in. This is my senior pilot, Warren. We all just call him Wings. He's the best. Flew fighter jets for Uncle Sam for twenty-two years and then came home to work in the family business. We're very fortunate to have him with us. He can find your boat if anyone can. Sit down, sit down. Can we get you anything? Drinks, food? I know you must be tired."

"Frank, you are far too gracious. I'm embarrassed by your generosity."

"Never underestimate the value of true friendship, Les. What you do for others will come to reward you many times over. You may not see it or believe that at first, but you live by that motto and you'll see I am right. You helped Vinny not wanting anything in return and now look. It's already paying off for you. Friends, that's the most important thing you can have in life. That and family. Am I right, Vinny?"

"Absolutely, Frank. God's truth."

Wings spread out a map of the coast of Georgia, South Carolina, and Northern Florida on the large mahogany coffee table. He had red circles drawn in numerous spots on the coast. Each circle had a number inside of it. He started to explain what he had done. "Each circle represents a possible offloading spot for product. A sailboat such as *Last Dance* will need at least eight feet of water to feel comfortable getting in and out. Docks with that approach depth or more would be even better. You know they're not going to take any chances on getting stuck on the bottom with millions of dollars' worth of hot product on board. They ain't going to call Sea Tow to come pull them off. The number in the circle indicates the order of which ones I think are the best choices for them. Number one is the best and twelve is the least desirable. I'm betting they've already docked with the mother ship, maybe a sub, and offloaded the product onto the sailboat. They probably gutted the sloop and threw everything overboard to make room for the product."

Essie, alarmed at that said, "If I get my hands on them, I'll kill them."

"You're our kind of woman, Essie. You might just get your chance. Okay, where was I? Oh yeah. I'm willing to bet that they are going to put in at one of these top twelve places."

Frank looked at Wings. "So what do you think we need to do? We can't be in twelve places at once."

"That's right, Frank. However, this is a big tidal region. They're going to come in with the incoming tide and go back out on an outgoing tide. Otherwise they'll move at a snail's pace and have to worry about water depth as well. Actually, I think one of the top five circles here is probably where they'll wind up putting in. They're going to want to be close to the interstate where a tractor trailer can make a quick exit. They're going to want to load up and get the hell out of the state. Marty will be here on the chopper soon. He's had the pontoons installed so he can do a water landing. We'll be able to go up and down the coast pretty damned quick with that. We'll circulate some pictures of the boat if Les has some we can blow up. We'll check in with all the dock masters at the marinas and explain why it would be a very good thing for them to help us. We get word that the boat is offloaded and they're headed back out to sea to scuttle her, we'll take the jet and keep track of them 'til we can get the chopper out there. I'm betting they are offloading right about now. If we move fast, we can catch them before they head out."

Frank and Vinny nodded in approval.

"That all makes sense, Wings. You got all the help and equipment you need aboard?"

"Yes, sir. Even brought night vision goggles. We're going to get them. I'm sure of it."

"That's good, Wings. And listen, I've put out some feelers to business associates up and down the coast. I told them if they hear of any new shipments of product coming in at any port, they're to call me that moment. They think because they came in on a cruising sailboat instead of a high powered cigarette boat that no one will pay them any attention. Most of the time that might do it, but right now, they're just a very slow boat. Are we ready?"

"Yes, sir. Plane is refueled. Marty should already be over at the terminal with the chopper."

"Let's go then. Les, do you and Essie feel up to riding on the planes with us, sort of acting as spotters? One of you can ride on the chopper and the other on the jet."

"We'd love to. You up to it, Essie?"

"I wouldn't let you go without me. I'll ride on the jet though. Helicopters make me a little nervous."

"That's great. That way we have somebody on each aircraft who will recognize the boat."

"We could tell it was *Last Dance* from a mile away in the dark."

"Okay, let's get on this."

We drove back out to the airport. There was now a beautiful Jet Ranger six-passenger chopper painted in the same high gloss black as the jet. I ran over to the chopper and Essie went to the jet with Frank. Vinny, Wings and I lifted off first. It was super not having to worry about runway space. We lifted off almost vertically. I turned to see the sleek black Cessna Citation clearing the end of the runway. They would be working the coast as we visited the top choice marinas.

As we approached Wings' number one choice, he circled twice to make sure the harbor was not busy and then set the chopper down dead center. We taxied over to the dock and tied up much like I would have done with a boat. We went to the dock master's office. Vinny looked at me.

"Okay, Les, you're going to wait out here while we talk with the manager. You can look around the harbor and see if you spot your boat. We need to ask this guy a few questions and having fewer folks around relaxes them more. That makes it easier for them to remember."

"Whatever you say, Vinny."

This particular harbor seemed too busy with pleasure boats for anyone to offload marijuana without everybody seeing. Unless they did it in the middle of the night, this would not be a good spot. As Vinny and Wings walked out of the dock master's office I could hear him in the background.

"Don't worry about a thing, Vinny. If I hear or see anything you will be the first, the very first person that I call. Yes, sir, Vinny. I'm on your side buddy. Glad to be of assistance. I hope I find them for you. Come back any time. I'll have a free slip for you. You can use my boat, even stay at my house, yes, sir. Just give me a call."

Wings looked over at Vinny, "Nice guy, eh?"

"Yeah. Great guy."

I quizzed Vinny, "You knew him?"

"Not directly. We knew some of the same people. It's a really small world. You know, it's that old six degrees of separation you hear about?"

"Oh, yeah. I've heard about that."

"Well, in our world it's more like one degree of separation. We deal with a lot of people, just about everywhere. Our friends have friends, et cetera, et cetera."

"I think I read you. No luck here, huh?"

"Nope, no sailboats docking here for several days. He says it's more of a powerboat harbor. We'll move on to the next place."

After visiting four more areas where a boat could dock and offload at night without drawing a lot of attention, I was starting to think it was either too late or the drug runners had a better plan than we anticipated. Vinny leaned over to me and practically yelled so I could hear him over the noise of the helicopter motor. "Change of direction. We have a development."

The chopper turned sharply and flew very low over the coast. Ahead I could see an island covered in palms with a runway down the middle of it. We landed next to Frank's jet which was already on the runway. Vinny and I went over to meet him.

"Vinny, I think we have a possible breakthrough. My good friend Sylvester, whom you know very well, says he wants to do us a favor."

"Sylvester! That's the son of a bitch that had his guys throw me in the drink. I'd love to get my hands on him."

"Now, Vinny. Sylvester feels remorse about that. He says he never wanted any harm to come you and that some of his boys got carried away. Something about a poker game and someone thinking someone else might be cheating."

"That's a lie. I never cheat at nothing."

"I know that, Vinny. However, that's in the past now. Sylvester says he has local knowledge on the who and where this load of product is headed. He'll be here in a minute. Let's hear what he has to say."

"I ain't happy about this, Frank. But, you're the boss and I'll always do what you say. You know that."

"I never question your loyalty, Vinny, never."

Frank walked slowly over to a concrete picnic bench alongside the runway where observers could sit and watch the planes take off and land on this exclusive private strip. He reached in his pocket and pulled out a large cigar. Before he could blink, one of his men produced a lighter and fired it up for him. He leaned back, took a deep puff, and watched as the smoke billowed up over his head. He had bearing and a real strong aura of power and influence. He was not someone to tangle with. He looked my way and motioned for me to come sit by him.

"Cigar, Les?"

"I'm sorry, Frank, but I don't smoke. Never have. My dad died of lung cancer and I have never wanted to try it after that."

"I understand completely. You have missed out on one of life's great rewards though. Nothing quite as rewarding as a great cigar. I have these brought in from Cuba."

"They're illegal in the States, aren't they?"

"That's funny, Les. You do have a sweet, innocent quality about you. I like you. Maybe we can do some business together when this little problem is resolved. I'm enjoying the excitement. I always loved boats. I've had a couple. I have one now in Miami at my house there but I haven't actually been on it in over a year. Just been too busy."

"What kind of a boat is it?"

"Not a sailboat, even though I think they're beautiful. Too slow for me. My boat is a Feadship. About a hundred fifty feet I think. Really nice. Costs like hell to keep it up. But the old lady enjoys having friends out for dinner on it when we're in Miami so I hang onto it. You'll have to see it when you're in Miami."

"I'd love to."

"Well, here comes Sylvester's plane."

"He's got a jet too?"

"Naw. He's got one of those little twin engine propeller jobs. Looks like Sky King's plane to me. It's cute but slow. If I can't get there quicker than I can on Delta, then why bother? Get my drift?"

"Yes, sir."

A beautifully restored Beechcraft Baron landed and taxied right up to the same area where Frank's plane was parked. It might be smaller and slower than Frank's but it was still a piece of aviation art and absolutely gorgeous in my book. The cabin gangplank was lowered and a young woman exited. In fact, she looked like she had just stepped out of Playboy Magazine. Behind her was Sylvester. He was old, grey, and stooped over. I could see the sun reflecting off the gold necklace and Rolex watch from fifty feet away.

He spotted Frank and walked straight to him.

"Frank, my friend, my very good friend. How good to see you."

"And you, Sylvester. How long has it been?"

"Too long, Frank. Much too long. I can't tell you how pleased I am that you called me about this. I'm glad I can be of some help to an old friend in troubled times such as these. Are we free to talk?"

"Let's go over there to the bench. Les, Vinny, we'll need a few minutes of privacy."

They walked like two generals meeting on the battlefield discussing strategy. They spoke quietly and gentlemanly from all appearances. They nodded and smiled several times and then stood up, shook hands, and walked away from each other. Sylvester went straight to his plane where his young friend was waiting for him. In less than five minutes they were airborne. Frank gathered

us all together in the main cabin of his jet. As I entered, I saw
Essie sitting in a plush leather swivel chair with what looked like a
Cosmo in her hand.

"Hey, Essie. What do you think?"

"Cappy, I think I'm ready to get out of sailing and buy a plane,
like this one."

"I know. I'm feeling poor. Let's see what Frank has to say."

Frank sat down in one of the other three swivel chairs.

"Here's the situation. Sylvester says none of the people
involved are his but he knows who they are and how they operate.
He says he wants to help us out as a favor to me. That undoubtedly
means these guys are competitors and he would like nothing more
than to see them go away for good. He thinks we might be
instrumental in making that happen. Anyway, here's how they
operate, according to Sylvester. They usually steal a boat just like
they've done with yours and bring it in after dark to a small private
boat yard up the Brunswick River. It's a place that's normally just a
work yard for shrimp boats. It's about eight miles up the river and
if the boat is there we'll be able to approach them and try to work
this out like gentlemen. After all, I don't care how they make their
living; we just want your boat back. Am I right, Les? Essie?"

"Yes, sir. We would be thrilled to get it back."

"And, as a concession to Sylvester, we'll explain to them why
this is not a good place for them to do business, ever again. Vinny,
you take several of the boys here and check out this boat yard. I'll
take Essie and we'll be waiting at the terminal in Brunswick. You
know how to handle this, right?"

"Frank, you know I do."

"I do. Good luck. Now, Essie, let's go back over to the jet and
we'll take a more relaxed look at the coast while we fly back. I do
love the ocean."

Frank took off and moments later we were airborne as well. Vinny sat up front next to Marty to help look for the place. Tank, two associates – as they like to call themselves – and I sat in the back. Even though we were headed toward a meeting with a very ruthless group of thugs, I marveled at how calm everyone aboard was. It couldn't have been a more relaxed group if we were all flying off to watch a baseball game. The guys talked about upcoming vacations and how well their kids were doing in grade school. I was more nervous than all of them added together.

Again we flew very low; not much over tree height. I could see Vinny squeezing the arm rest in the front seat. He looked at Marty. "Marty, do we have to fly this low? I mean, we could hit a power line or something. It makes me nervous."

"Relax, Vinny. I've been flying like this since Nam. Reminds me of flying over the Mekong Delta. I just follow the path of the river. We should be there in the next couple of minutes."

We all looked out the windows and finally saw a small boatyard with three large shrimp boats tied up to the wharf. There was a ramshackle building beside the dock, a few trucks in the gravel parking lot and that was all. *Last Dance* wasn't there. Marty started to hover over the turning basin.

"I'm going to set down out in the middle and taxi over to the dock. Vinny, you going to go in and talk to them?"

"Yeah, Tank and I will go together."

Marty eased us over to a place where the chopper blades where higher than the dock and threw a single line around a piling. Vinny and Tank hopped out and walked toward the building. In the doorway, a guy who looked like a cross between Grizzly Adams and a TV wrestler stood staring at us. He was wearing only bib overalls and white rubber boots. He looked like a fight waiting to happen. There was no hesitation from Tank or Vinny as they

approached him. He looked for just a moment as if he was going
to block their entrance and then he just jumped back out of their
way. They certainly were persuasive when they were on a mission.
In about ten minutes they exited the building. This time, two other
guys who appeared to be clones of the first stepped out, held the
door open for Vinny and Tank, and then stopped on the porch
while they returned to where we were waiting.

They hopped aboard. Vinny looked at us. "Everybody back on
the chopper. We don't have any time to spare. Your boat was here
and left with the outgoing tide about three hours ago. They
normally run out about fifteen miles and scuttle them so we have
to hurry. They have to be getting close to that distance by now."

Marty lifted off like a police chopper following a stolen car. He
kept the chopper at a thousand feet and we had good visibility, so
if *Last Dance* was anywhere close to fifteen miles out we should
be able to spot her. It's extremely difficult to spot anything at sea
from the air. We could see the wakes of large fishing boats on the
water but sailboats don't leave much of a trail. We spotted several
sailboats and descended to check them out.

"I really don't think they would have the sails up to run out here
and sink her. I doubt they even know how to sail a boat. They'll
just fire the diesel up and… There she is!"

Just off to our right sat *Last Dance*. She was not moving and no
sails were up. She had a large speedboat tied up next to her. They
had to be getting ready to sink her. Marty descended low over top
of them and it became apparent they had automatic weapons and
were not about to put up with any intruders moving in on their
operation.

Vinny turned to Tank, "Tank, go to the bag."

"I'm on it."

Tank produced a canvas bag from behind the back seat in the storage area. It wasn't very large and even though I was thinking they were going to pull out some guns, it just wasn't big enough to contain any. I watched in disbelief as Tank withdrew two hand grenades. I had been exposed to them in the military so there was no question as to what I was seeing. Tank took one in his right hand and looked over at me.

"Flash grenade. This goes off over them they'll have trouble remembering what it is they're doing. Really neat ordnance. Okay Vinny, I'm ready. What do you want to do?"

"Marty will get you over top of them, just off to the side. Pull the pin and drop it just off to the side of their speedboat away from the sailboat. I don't want to hurt the sailboat or kill anybody. We just want to let them know we're in the driver's seat here and unless they want to swim home they better pay attention."

Marty positioned the helicopter precisely and Tank dropped the first grenade. It exploded just before hitting the water and shrapnel shattered the window on their speed boat. It produced an incredible noise and blinding flash. They started ducking and screaming profanities at us. Marty picked up his mike and held it out the window so they could see he wanted to talk. He quickly reached them on the marine channel. He was point blank with them.

"We don't want you or have anything to do with your business. We want the sailboat. Just back away from it, get on your powerboat and leave it. Do not sink it. You have thirty seconds before the next grenade will be dropped directly on you."

Two men literally jumped off the sailboat and into the speedboat. It took off toward the open ocean at fifty miles per hour. Vinny smiled at Tank.

"Nice job. Now Marty, let's make sure they are completely out of sight and not turning around. Les, if we drop you and Tank aboard, can you make it back to Brunswick?"

"No question about it Vinny. Where will we meet up?"

"Stop at the first nice marina you come to and Tank will give me a call. We'll come pick you up."

"Vinny."

"What?"

"We owe you big time. Words can't express how strongly I feel about that. You have a friend for life. All of you guys. If I can ever help you in any way..."

"Like Frank said, Les. Friends are what we're all about. I'll call Essie and give her the good news. You guys make a beeline for port."

The chopper set down right beside *Last Dance* and we boarded her. She was a complete wreck below but I was able to get the motor started and the GPS running. We could get her in.

After we got a heading, I went below to take a look at how bad they had messed her up. I was floored by what I saw. In order to fill the entire boat up with marijuana and whatever else they were smuggling, they had literally ripped out the entire interior. The settees, the galley, the salon table, even the freezer box and stove. The outside looked fine but they had done more damage to the inside of the boat than it was worth. It would certainly cost more to repair than the boat could even be sold for.

In spite of all this, she was our home and we'd just have to make do. Tank looked below and was astounded as well.

"Man, I'm sorry. I can't believe those bastards did this much damage. Can you fix it back?"

"I'll have to. I don't have the money and I'm not much of a carpenter but maybe I can get somebody who's better than me to help with it. Right now, I just don't know. I hate to show this to Essie. She'll be sick about it."

We got in to the marina just before dark. Tank had called as we got close and there was a car waiting to take us back to the hotel. I was completely drained in every way. Neither Essie nor I had had four hours sleep in the past two days. I was not looking forward to breaking the news to her.

When we walked in the hotel, Wings met us in the lobby and took us up to Frank's suite. Essie was there along with a couple of his associates waiting for us to get in. She got up and rushed over to the door and hugged me. "Cappy, this is so exciting. We got *Last Dance* back? Is she okay?"

"Well, she looks okay from the outside but I'm not sure she can be saved, at least I don't know if we will be able to do it."

"What's wrong?"

"She's basically been gutted. The entire interior was removed and trashed to get stowage room below for the crap they were smuggling."

"Oh, baby. I'm sorry. Are you alright?"

"I'm more concerned about you."

"Don't you worry about me. I'll be fine. I'll help and we'll get her put back together. You'll see. It will all work out."

"I love your optimism. I wish I had more of it. I guess I'm just really tired."

I walked over to Frank. "I can't thank you enough for all the trouble and expense you've gone through to help us. We are not wealthy people and can't begin to reimburse you for all the planes, fuel, and time. I know it had to cost a ton of money to do all this. Is there anything I can do?"

"You did it when you saved Vinny. You didn't ask for anything from him when you pulled him aboard and let him stay with you 'til he was safe. Vinny and I are family and when you did that for him you did it for me as well. It is an honor to help you, not a favor. What else can I do that will help you and Miss Essie get back on your feet?"

"I guess we need to head back to North Carolina as soon as we can. I'll make arrangements to leave the boat here 'til I can figure out what to do with her. And I've come to one conclusion that there's something I have to do and I need to do it immediately."

"What's that, Cappy?"

"Essie and I are going to go home and get married. My divorce is final. I'm a free man and there's no reason why we shouldn't do it right now. And you are all invited to the wedding. I don't know where it will be in New Bern or exactly what day but it will be very soon. I hope you'll come and help us to celebrate."

"Les, you and Essie can count on it. I'll bring my wife, and Vinny, even Tank and Wings if they want to come. If you need any help, or want us to give somebody a ride into town on the jet, you just call."

Frank raised his glass. "A toast to Essie and Les. May you have many happy years together."

Everyone raised a glass while Essie and I embraced. At the end of a very trying time, it was a tremendous moment. We went to our room and literally crashed and burned. We didn't get up 'til almost lunch. While we were dressing the phone rang. It was Vinny.

"Les, Frank says to come down to the restaurant and join us for lunch. He will be leaving around two and if you can be ready he'll drop you off at the airport in New Bern."

"That's great news. We're almost ready. We'll be down in about ten minutes. Thanks."

Essie looked beautiful after a full night's sleep. Having set the plan to get married in concrete didn't seem to have any effect on her at all. She was as loving and compassionate as ever, even more so. I could feel inside that this was the right move. I wouldn't say I wasn't nervous because I was. My first marriage certainly left a lot of doubts about the entire institution in my mind. Essie had eased those doubts and I knew I didn't want to keep going down the road without her. We entered the restaurant and saw Frank and Vinny over at a corner table. They both stood to greet us. "Good morning our soon-to-be newlyweds. How did you sleep?"

"Frank, Vinny, we are finally rested. The last four days were a struggle. We are fortunate to be here, to be together, and to have friends like you. Is it true you're willing to give us a plane ride back to New Bern?"

"Of course. I wouldn't have it any other way. Please, sit down and get something to eat. Now that the trauma of your boat being stolen is over, tell me a little about yourselves. How did you meet and what drew you to each other?"

Essie answered first. "Frank, it's almost been a fairytale with a few nightmares thrown in for good measure. The common ingredient through the whole thing has been boats. We both love boats and sailing and the other people who are drawn to it. We seem to all have something in common. I was born in Texas but in my early teens we moved to Wisconsin for my Dad's job. I hated the winters up there and after a disastrous teenage wedding,

I wound up in North Carolina. That was over twenty years ago and I'm still there. I still love Texas though. If I ever leave North Carolina, that's where I'd go."

It was then my turn. "I'm from Virginia. I went to college in North Carolina and I've basically been here ever since. I love the coast of North Carolina but I have to say I'm drawn to the tropics and wouldn't mind spending the winters on a sailboat in the Keys or the Bahamas."

Frank looked at us both square into our eyes as he asked a serious question. "So, you think you have finally found your soul mate? This is the person you want to spend the rest of your days with, eh?"

We both assured him it was.

"I like you both a lot. I want you to call me Uncle Frank from here on out. And I think I have a wedding gift for you that you will both appreciate."

"Frank, I mean Uncle Frank. You don't have to give us anything. You've already done so much and you coming to our wedding is more than we could ever ask of you."

"Nonsense. I want my gift to be the most special one you get. So, I want you to draw something out for me, and take your time. Get some old pictures or brochures if you have them. I want you to show me how you want your boat fixed back up. There's a famous boatyard down this way we use for our boat. They take care of my Feadship and they do incredible work. I'll have your boat moved to their yard while you're at home getting married. I'll get with them and pay to have your boat fixed back just like you want and maybe throw in a few newer gadgets and stuff while they're at it."

"Frank, Uncle Frank. You've got to be kidding! We couldn't begin to let you do that. It would cost a ton to get all that work done."

"A ton to you, maybe a few pounds to me. I have more money than I can ever spend responsibly. I do this for you and it makes me feel good. That's what my money buys for me. You would do the same I'm sure."

Essie got up, ran around the table and gave Frank a hug I thought might choke him. "You are the best uncle anyone could ever imagine. You will always be welcome at our house."

Vinny looked at Essie sheepishly. "What am I? Chopped liver? I'm in line here too, you know?"

"Vinny, I could never forget you. Picking you up out of the water has been one of the best things we ever did."

Vinny got the hug he was hoping for. We finished lunch and as we tried to check out, we discovered that Uncle Frank had also sprung for the hotel. I couldn't help but wonder how it would feel to have enough money to be able to do these sorts of things for people you cared about. I would love to try it out.

We landed in New Bern by dinner time. Frank and Vinny continued on to Ohio. We certainly understood that Frank and Vinny's family might have some interests that we didn't want to know about. However, the way they treated us clearly showed they had a good side and friends and family were very important to them. We would reserve any judgment about them and base our relationship on the way they had treated us. Over the years we would read some newspaper articles related to Uncle Frank but he was never indicted or prosecuted for anything and, for the most part, kept a very low profile. If he was a crook, he was the best crook around.

12

My memories of my first wedding were those of a very stress-filled period. There were tons of people I didn't know, lots of standing and shaking hands and pretending to be thrilled with what was going on. The truth is, I was scared shitless and glad when it was finally over. I didn't want my wedding to Essie to be anything like that. I would try my best to make everything about it wonderful and make sure she got the kind of wedding young girls dream of.

Her first wedding had been a shotgun affair. She was a pregnant seventeen-year-old marrying a guy she barely knew and who would walk her down a path that would become totally unbearable. Her first husband fell into a world of addictions and failure that dragged her and her much loved children along for the ride. By the time she left him, she was in her late thirties and burned out. She still believed in marriage and wanted ours to be the way she always dreamed it should be. I would do my part. She literally beamed as she went about planning her wedding day. Her close friends would join her for brainstorming sessions that I'm sure she enjoyed almost as much as the wedding itself. They would meet, open a bottle of wine, sit out on the patio, and talk about the things women like to talk about.

I started playing two nights a week at Captain Ratty's to keep some money coming in and the rest of the time I took some small jobs working on boats. We agreed that we liked the original layout of *Last Dance* and wanted her put back the way she was when she was new. The yard said they had a copy of the original specifications and some manufacturer's pictures of the interior to go by. We picked out fabric colors and that was about all that was needed from us. We were extremely happy that this work was being done. Knowing she would be ready by the time the wedding was over just added another level of excitement to our anticipation.

Helen had been living by herself in the new house Lou built just before he passed on. She invited us to stay in her guest room until the wedding was over and we shoved off for the third time.

We planned the wedding date only thirty days out. We knew it was short but we were anxious to get on with our lives and head back to *Last Dance*. We would have loved to drive down and check on her progress but we couldn't break free during this hectic time.

Jim and Sara decided to host an engagement party for us on board *The Lone Ranger*. It would be a small affair with only ten couples attending. The guests were our closest friends in New Bern and they were as happy with our upcoming marriage as we were. They picked us all up at the Sheraton Grande marina dock and motored out into the Neuse River to an anchorage just off Union Point. It was a very quiet, warm evening with a ten knot breeze. That was just enough to keep the no-see-ums from eating us alive and cool things down so that sitting in the cockpit was comfortable. Ten couples were more than would fit in the cockpit so several guests walked around the decks and found comfortable places to sit. Jim turned up the cockpit speakers with our favorite,

Luis Miguel, singing the most romantic Latin tunes ever. Essie, Sara, and Leigh mixed cocktails and made several plates of cheese, crackers, chips and dip for everyone. More than a few bottles of wine were opened and the guys attacked the Corona with a passion. All the guests had heard one version or another of our adventure with the drug runners and wanted the full story straight from the horses' mouths. Even though it had been hell living through the ordeal, I could see that telling the story in years to come would be quite entertaining. It was a story that needed no embellishment to be exciting. The guests stayed glued to every word and had a slew of questions when we were done. Essie and I separated our parts of the story and helped each other if we left out any worthy detail. The part about the sharks circling us always got everyone going. I didn't tell them that I'd woken up several nights since we got back in a cold sweat with dreams of sharks bumping my legs as I hung off the dinghy. That memory remains very fresh for me and hopefully will fade in time.

As the evening wore down, the women gathered in one area to talk about wedding gowns, flowers, wedding cakes, and grandbabies. The guys talked boats, beer, and more boats. The night was glorious and if it lasted forever it would not have been too long. Great evening, wonderful friends, a quiet anchorage on a tremendous boat. I know of no better place to be.

The day of the wedding approached quickly. Essie had a number of family members I had never met flying in from Texas and Oklahoma. My mother, a long-time widow, my sister, her husband, my brother, and his wife were coming in for the wedding. We had chosen Centenary United Methodist Church in New Bern for the service and the Chelsea Restaurant just a short walk down the street for the reception. The church was very old and the stone building looked like a castle out of the hills of

Scotland. It had two separate sanctuaries, one large enough for several hundred people and a more intimate chapel that had room for a little less than one hundred people. Though we weren't members at the time, the church was very gracious to allow us to hold the service there. We actually had several churches in town that wanted to rent us a sanctuary for up to five thousand dollars for the day. I'm sorry, but I just couldn't see Jesus taking that course. I'm firmly convinced he would do everything possible to get couples to marry in his church and encourage them to join thereafter.

The small chapel featured incredible stained glass windows. The limited number of people it could comfortably hold was forcing us to be very selective about whom we invited as we could easily have doubled that with friends that we knew would come. We just explained to everyone it would be a small, mostly family affair. Between Essie's family, mine, good friends, and our new friends in Ohio, it was going to be a tight fit. Susanne was enjoying all the moments associated with putting the ceremony together from the flowers to the place settings for the reception. We didn't want a long formal ceremony. She planned that the service would take less than thirty minutes and then a horse-drawn carriage would pick us up in front of the chapel and drive us to The Chelsea.

I was ecstatic to have made her so happy. We had been together for over a year and had never experienced a cross word between us. She was an upbeat, positive person who was thankful for all life had given her, and she tried her best to instill that in me. If that wasn't always possible, she at least was thankful on my behalf. I couldn't ask for nor find a more perfect soul mate.

The night before our wedding we had a reception upstairs in Captain Ratty's. Tom let us have the room for free and discounted all the food to the point I was embarrassed to accept it. But he insisted, so we held it there. That night I ate something that didn't sit well with me, and I stayed up the entire night fighting off intestinal turmoil. I got less than an hour's sleep before I was supposed to be at a breakfast reception held in honor of our families at the church. I somehow drug myself out of bed, got dressed, and faked my way through it. I told Essie what was going on and she insisted I go to the hotel room we had rented for the night and sleep a couple of hours before the wedding. I crashed immediately and had trouble getting up to make the ceremony. After I got my tux on and some coffee in me, I started to feel better.

As I entered the chapel for the five p.m. ceremony, it was amazing to see that there was standing room only. Everybody in the world who was important in our lives had made the trip. A lot of those in my family knew how difficult my first marriage had been. They were very happy for me knowing that I had found someone like Essie. They all loved her immediately. Essie's family seemed to like me okay but I had the feeling they wished she had found someone a little closer to her age. I understood where they were coming from and could deal with it. After all, they lived out west. As the introductory music started, I went to the front of the chapel and stood beside the pastor. He was a young man named Danny and he seemed genuinely delighted to be joining us in marriage.

I hadn't seen Essie since she had left for the chapel and never in her wedding gown. It was a very special moment when the organist started playing the regal "Trumpet Voluntary." Wow, did Essie look beautiful, with her dark hair, white form-fitting gown, and spectacular smile walking toward me. Her father Jim held her arm and brought her over to me where he volunteered to the pastor that he was the one to give her away. I took her hand and the rest was magic. After pronouncing us married and we kissed, the audience gave us a huge round of applause. As we exited the chapel, the crowd held up a number of large, brightly colored umbrellas in the light rain. The umbrellas combined with the many different dress colors and the translucent bubbles they were blowing, it was almost like being part of a Disney movie.

Happiest of Days

We climbed aboard the carriage and moved off slowly for a ride through town and on to The Chelsea.

When we arrived at our reception, we were again applauded and greeted by all our friends as they encircled the newest Mr. and Mrs. in the room. This had to be the most diverse group of people ever assembled on the planet. There were real cowboys right off the ranch from Texas, my family from Virginia who were all very reserved, Essie's family, sailing friends, a movie star, doctors, lawyers, and probably even an Indian chief. There were men in military dress uniforms, suits, blue jeans, and even kilts. I had to admit that we hung out with many different types of people. Near the end of the reception line was none other than Uncle Frank and Vinny. Frank introduced his beautiful wife, Gayle, and Vinny had brought his wife, Sandy. We were shocked to see that Sandy was very tall and slender as opposed to Vinny who was exactly the opposite. Both wives were gracious and hugged us while telling Essie how beautiful she was and how much they loved the ceremony. Essie had placed names on the individual tables to best match up the guests with people she felt would enjoy their company the most. Some tables were full of close friends and others were couples who had never met but Essie thought they should. One such mixed table was set for Uncle Frank, Vinny, and their wives. Essie had matched them up with Grimshaw, Sara, David, and Leigh. That promised to be a lively group. I wished we could have spent the entire evening there listening in, but we had to mingle and share time with all our guests. The meal was delicious as is always the case with the Chelsea.

For entertainment, our dear friend Carmine Stabile, sang for the entire evening. He could do all the great romantic voices like Sinatra, Dean Martin, the entire Rat Pack, and then venture out into such diverse acts as Stevie Wonder, Garth Brooks or the Eagles. He provided a wonderful night of music and we all stayed until the Chelsea had to close for the night. I hated for the night to end. It was a truly a magical affair. Essie and I went back to the hotel and spent our first night together as husband and wife.

"Cappy, you okay? You wondering 'What the hell did I do?'"

"Not a chance. I'm the winner here. I got the beautiful young woman. She's hot looking, talented, loving and she likes sailing. You, on the other hand, got the bald, older, slightly overweight, bespectacled guy who also loves sailing."

"Sorry, but that's not who I see. I see a twenty-five-year-old, John Wayne type of guy who's forced to age some against all his efforts. You will live to be a hundred and I'll be right there to make sure you do. And you will be treated to more of the hottest episodes in the bedroom than anybody you ever knew. And I want to get that started right now. Just lay on back, big guy."

"I don't know what I did in a previous life to deserve you, but I am not going to question it."

The night and next morning went by spectacularly. We spent the afternoon visiting with out-of-town relatives. Around six we met Uncle Frank, Vinny, and their wives upstairs at Ratty's. When we walked in, we saw that their entourage had picked up a lot of new members. There was Grimshaw and Sara, David, Leigh, Tom, and Karen. They were in full swing. The party had started without us.

"Oh man, the rowdiest group we know has consolidated into one very large group. New Bern is in trouble."

"You don't know the half of it. Didn't you say you guys were going to go to Key West for your honeymoon?"

"That's right. We fly down this evening."

"We're all going to Florida too. So you go to Key West and after you and Miss Essie burn yourselves out for several days, you drive back to Miami to my place and join this group there for another couple of days."

"Uncle Frank, you're taking this whole group to Miami?"

"That's right. We're taking my plane down tonight and my boat out tomorrow. What fun is it to have a place like mine if you have to hang around in it by yourself? You got a great bunch of friends here and we're just going to share them with you for a while."

"Sounds like you guys will have more fun than we will. We're jealous."

Frank's wife Gayle beamed as she made a very gracious offer. "Essie, you can have a key to our place down there and whenever you and Cappy are in Florida, bingo. You'll have a great place to hang your hat."

Essie walked over to Gayle and hugged her. She kissed Uncle Frank on the cheek. "Gayle, you're a lucky woman. He's a keeper."

"Tell me about it. Of course, I've been keeping him for about forty years. I know where all the rusted spots are."

Everyone laughed throughout dinner and by seven thirty Essie and I had to go to the airport to catch our plane. The rest of the group was still going strong when we left.

"You know, Essie, I want to get us a jet like Frank's so we can come and go whenever we want; not have to worry about bags, security, or airline schedules."

"Yeah, if only it didn't cost twenty thousand bucks a month to keep it, the pilot, and the hangar going, I'd be right there with you. It's probably not going to happen anytime soon. Keep buying Powerball tickets."

13

We arrived at the Fort Lauderdale airport around ten thirty and picked up a rental car. The ride down the highway through the Keys was about four more hours so we decided to spend the first night with friends, Jack and Lorraine Miller, on their trawler, *Mystic Knights*. Only an old fart such as me understood the humor in the boat name. It was the name of the lodge that was featured on the early 50s comedy "Amos and Andy": the Mystic Knights of the Sea Lodge. Jack and Lorraine were expecting us. They lived aboard the trawler at a small marina in Key Largo. When we arrived they had us aboard for a celebratory nightcap and said they knew we had to be tired so they would tuck us in and we could socialize in the morning over breakfast.

"That would be great. We are really tired. Which berths do you want us to sleep in?"

Jack replied, "You're not staying aboard. We have a surprise for you. The marina has a small guest cottage that they are going to let you stay in tonight. I'll show you in."

We walked over to the marina office and around the back was a small addition made of cinderblocks. It didn't look like much on the outside but inside it was lovely. There on the dinette table were a dozen red roses that my sister had sent ahead of us. I don't know how she knew where we would be staying, but she had always been a very thoughtful sister and loved doing things like this. Essie was touched. Jack and Lorraine had also placed a bottle of champagne on the table with a very nice card. We thanked them for their thoughtfulness and then collapsed.

"I promise you this is the last marriage and honeymoon I'll ever do. I'm worn slam out."

"Trust me, Cappy. This is your last marriage. You know when I took that vow that said 'Til death do us part'?"

"Yes. Why?"

"You didn't even have to say it. I said it for both of us. You try to leave, you're dead!"

"Well, that's pretty straightforward."

"That's just the kind of girl I am. Now slide on over here and I'll rub your old bald head."

A hot Florida sun pouring in through the blinds woke us up. We were also excited we would be visiting Key West. We had a wonderful breakfast aboard *Mystic Knights* with Jack and Lorraine. They said they were soon moving to Alabama on the Gulf coast. They had bought a small farm that bordered a river where they could still live aboard while they built a house. I don't know why anyone would move away from a place as beautiful as the Keys, but we promised to visit them there when we could.

Shortly after breakfast, Essie and I took the rental car and headed toward Key West, about three hours south. The drive is drop-dead beautiful with the Gulf of Mexico and its bright green water to the right and the neon blue Atlantic to the left. The colors are incredibly vibrant and the land on either side of the road is so narrow at times you could spit from one body of water to the other. Granted, there are tourist traps every fifteen feet but at least they are mostly boat or diving oriented so I enjoy looking at them. There's a lot of little hole-in-the-wall restaurants and bars that looked like they should all have "Welcome Home, Les" signs on them. I loved the drive.

When we arrived in Key West, we checked into the little bed and breakfast I found on the internet, the Duval House Inn. It was actually a small cluster of old Victorian cottages that encircled a pool and cabana house. Each cottage was a room with a luxurious bathroom. They were each decorated in a tropical motif and meticulously maintained. The courtyard the cottages shared was full of lush palm trees, live oaks, and vines. As you walked through thick vegetation occasional small clearings would open up with a bench or chairs for a couple to enjoy some private time. As hot as the outside was, it was always felt cool in the shady courtyard. Being on a shoestring budget, we had rented the smallest cottage for three nights. We napped and relaxed around at the Inn for a few hours then around four we started to walk down Duval Street.

We would make our first Duval Crawl as the locals call it. Key West, at least in the commercial area around Duval Street, is a very unique city. It's comprised of two hundred bars separated by gift shops. It's the ultimate party city. In most towns there are laws against walking the street with an open alcoholic beverage container. In Key West, many of the bars have windows that open to the sidewalks, where you can buy a drink and carry it while you're walking. Toleration of all things is the basic theme of the town. I was fascinated by the poster asking everyone to be sure to attend the Drag Races that weekend. The poster had no pictures of cars, just good looking women. Essie explained to me that she had heard about this before. The race consisted of guys dressed in drag pushing grocery carts down the street in high heels and gowns. Only in Key West.

We walked to the end of Duval Street and discovered what would become my favorite bar in the entire world, Schooner's Wharf. It was old but its enclosed courtyard and covered bar overlooking the harbor made up for the minimal decor. Docked in front of it were four large schooners that took tourists out on sunset and champagne cruises around the Key West bight. One was the *America* that Essie and I had almost destroyed when she fell overboard in Beaufort. The crew remembered her as we walked over to the dock where she was moored. One of them yelled out to the others, "Look, it's the lady who did the somersault off her boat in Beaufort!" Essie took it very good naturedly and we decided to take a sail on one of the schooners that evening. We had been on the *America* before so we took the sunset cruise on the larger *Western Union*. We had a ringside seat as the *America* passed us at a speed of at least fourteen knots. She was a spectacular site. I discovered that day that I loved Key West. I don't think I could live there full-time but I would certainly entertain being on *Last Dance* there from January through March each winter. The climate would be great. There were palm trees everywhere and the town celebrates boats. What more could I ask?

The next morning we bought tickets on the fast cat to the Dry Tortugas. The fast cat is a seventy-five foot long motorized catamaran that can make the trip in a little over two hours. The Tortugas are a small group of islands located seventy miles southwest of Key West in the Gulf of Mexico. There's an old fort built on the island called Fort Jefferson. It's part of the National Parks system and is federally maintained. The Fort is so large that it covers almost every square inch of the island and is surrounded by some of the most beautiful turquoise water imaginable. It's deep blue and crystal clear. There's a protected anchorage right beside it and there were at least a dozen sailboats visiting there.

Though the water around the fort was shallow and clear, the water in the anchorage was obviously deeper, a dark blue color. I asked a Ranger whether you could snorkel off the boat in the lagoon. He said, "I wouldn't this time of year. The lagoon has a lot of tarpon in it right now and the hammerheads follow them here. There's some really huge ones out there."

No wonder I hadn't seen anyone diving off the sides of the boats. We did snorkel in the shallow areas close to shore. I pointed out a huge barracuda to Essie and she practically walked on water to get back to the beach. I promised her they wouldn't hurt her but she was more than a little intimidated by the way it seemed to be motionless in the water, yet always just ten feet away with those huge teeth, and staring at us.

The trip on the fast cat took the better part of the day and when we got back to Key West we were pretty tired. We wound up at the La Concha Hotel downtown watching sunset on their balcony. We wandered down to the main floor and spent a couple of hours listening to a trio called the Spectrelles. They were two gals in evening gowns, long white gloves and beehive hairdos flanking a guy in an Elvis-styled gold lamé jacket who sang doo-wop songs from the 50s. We enjoyed them immensely. It capped off a perfect day. We fell into the overstuffed bed back at the Duval House and stayed in bed almost until noon. Essie and I enjoyed talking with each other on almost any topic. There were very few things we didn't see eye to eye on. We spent the next evening eating at a nice restaurant and just walking the docks looking at boats. We both had the same thought at the same time. Essie looked over at me.

"Cappy, what are the chances we could run by the boatyard on the way home and see *Last Dance*? They have to be about done with her by now."

"Uncle Frank wanted us to spend a couple of days with them in Miami. Since our entire group is already there, I say we just plan on staying with him a couple nights and go to see the boat."

"Great idea."

Essie had a way of making sure that all of her ideas somehow became mine when she wanted me to do something. She is very smart. We drove up to Miami the next morning. We would always have fond memories of our honeymoon at the Duval House and hope, one day, we will revisit there for an anniversary trip.

I called Frank and got the address and basic directions to his home in Miami. The rental car had a GPS on the dash so we entered the street name and number and followed the voice instructions to Uncle Frank's house. First, using the word "house" to describe his place would be a huge understatement. Most of the homes on the street leading up to it had to cost ten million plus each. His was on the very end of the cul-de-sac and had decorated iron gates and brick columns that looked like you might be entering a university campus. We approached the gate and a camera turned to scan our car and then a voice came over a speaker mounted just under the camera. "Who's calling?"

"We are Les and Essie Pendleton from North Carolina."

"One moment, please."

In about ten seconds the voice directed us to drive forward as the gate opened. The house was straight out of "House Beautiful," the tropical edition. White stucco walls with a terracotta roof, a circular driveway in front, with a fountain in the center. A young man in crisp white shorts and a pressed shirt came out and directed me to leave the car where it was with the key in it and he would park it for us out of the sun. I have to say, I'd never been to a home with valet parking before. Essie was amazed. "Didn't Frank say this was just his weekend home?"

"He did."

"God, I can only imagine what his house in Ohio looks like. How much money does he have?"

"A lot more than us. Of course, that wouldn't take much but he's doing well, that's for sure."

We walked to the front door and as soon as the uniformed maid greeted us we could hear Grimshaw and Frank laughing in the background. Rosie, the housekeeper, escorted us to a large lanai area where Frank was entertaining his new collection of friends from New Bern. There was splashing behind them, and as we walked toward the group, they all jumped up and applauded the newlyweds. Frank came over, hugged us both and asked if we would like a drink. In seconds we were seated with them by the pool with a Painkiller in hand.

Grimshaw leaned over to me, "Les, even Beverly Hills doesn't have places like this in it. Check out his boat."

Just beyond the fence surrounding the property was the Miami canal system and the topsides of many large yachts could be seen over the fence. The largest yacht was the closest, and it was Frank's. It was a gleaming white Feadship, well over one hundred fifty feet long. I could see people in uniforms walking around on board, obviously his crew going about their duties. Just cleaning a boat like that would be a full-time job for a good sized crew.

"Damn, Jim. I've never felt so poor."

"Les, you know what they say about boats. The best kind to have is a friend's. Frank says we can go with him on *Buckeye* whenever he's down here."

"*Buckeye*?"

"Oh, yeah. He's a big Ohio State fan."

Gayle came over to Essie and invited her to take a tour of the house. She jumped at the chance. I was content to sit down for a while and join the guys as they sampled a few Coronas.

"How was Key West?"

"It was just about what I was expecting. I've never seen so many bars on one street in my life."

"Great, huh?"

"We'll go back. If we get to take the boat south this winter, we'll stop off there again for a few days. By the way, Frank, is there any chance we could drop over and see *Last Dance*?"

"I'm way ahead of you. You'll get to see her in the morning. I've got my chopper coming by here around noon and we'll all take a little trip to look her over."

Even though Frank's place was like a walled fortress, it was hard not to take notice of the three or four guys dressed like sports announcers in grey slacks and polo shirts as they observed everything going on inside and out of the huge mansion and grounds.

"Uncle Frank, do you really have to have guys around all the time to be safe?"

"You know, Les, it's like this: I probably don't but can I afford to take that chance? I've got kids, grandkids, and a loving wife that I think the world of, so I want to be around for a lot more years. I'm also responsible for their safety. In my career path, there's a lot of tough people. Some are completely dependable and I actually trust them with my life and that of my family. However, there's always some folks you wouldn't trust any more than you'd trust your Congressman or Senator. They'll do anything for money, and I do mean anything. They want power, and to be forthright about it, they want what I have and they'd do anything to take it from me. I've been around long enough to know that, and I'm just not willing to give anyone the opportunity. So, if that means I have to hire a few extra people to guarantee that we're safe, so be it. All it all, it ain't such bad a lifestyle. Am I right?"

"You are right there, Uncle Frank."

Uncle Frank and wife Gayle - The Albertinis

"And you, Les, you have something money can't buy. You have a wonderful group of loyal friends and now a wonderful wife. They are worth more than anything else on the planet. And Grimshaw, a great guy but what a mess. We're going to go see

him out in Hollywood. Jim has promised to give me and Gayle the full tour if we came out to his place."

Jim leaned over and responded, "Frank, you aren't going to see anything out there any nicer than you see here."

"Don't need to see houses. Gayle wants to see Jack Nicholson and Warren Beatty. You know them, don't you, Jim?"

"I do. Of course, getting them to take a minute to meet with some of my friends might not be all that easy. I'm a working actor and I've done a lot of films but I'm not at the level of Jack or Warren. It would be a big favor if they did this for me. I can't promise anything but I'll give it my best effort."

"I understand, Jim. By the way, aren't all you actors and actresses members of some kind of union?"

"It's called the Screen Actors Guild."

"That's right. I can probably give them a call and set something up if you strike out. Just let me know. Find out what's the best time for you and ask them. I'll be willing to bet you they'll jump on the chance to help you out."

"You know, Frank. I believe you when you say that. Hey, are we still going on the boat ride this evening?"

"We are. As soon as Gayle gets back with the ladies. I'll go ahead and tell the captain to fire up the engines. We'll look around the canals and then head out to Biscayne Bay for a nighttime ride and a little entertainment."

"Entertainment?"

"Yeah, I've got a little group coming over to play for us. There's room out on the lido deck for a little dancing as well. You know, guys, I really enjoy having folks down here. It's not much fun to roll around in a big old place like this with just me and the wife. We enjoy being together and all, but we love company. Gayle would rather throw a party than eat when she's hungry.

This is a great time for her. And you know the saying, 'if momma ain't happy, ain't nobody happy.'"

"Amen, Frank."

The girls returned wide-eyed. They had toured Gayle and Frank's estate and Essie said that the only place she had ever seen that would compare was Biltmore Estate in Asheville, North

Carolina. She said she liked Gayle's better since it was new and being lived in, not a museum like the Biltmore. Frank told the girls we'd be ready to shove off in thirty minutes. They all headed off to change clothes and the guys, well, we just had another beer. Life in Miami was good.

Uncle Frank's Miami "Cottage"

The captain and crew, about five of them, expertly guided *Buckeye* out of her slip. She was so big that you could barely hear the motors running unless you were near the stern where the exhaust was located. The captain steered from the control center located inside on the top deck. There was an outside steering station located on the bridge as well but he preferred the inside station. He was young, perhaps forty, and in every way a professional. The crew was even younger, mostly in their twenties, and all nattily attired in crisp white shirts and shorts. A close look at *Buckeye*'s custom logo showed an interesting touch. Instead of the typical Ohio state capital "O" with the namesake buckeye leaf on the bottom right corner, it had a palm tree substituted for it. That was the perfect touch.

Being aboard *Buckeye* felt like being on a cruise ship. There was also a cook and a bartender. The band joined us at the last minute and set their instruments up on the outside top deck. The group was made up of three guys who looked like Jamaicans. They brought a keyboard, a guitar and a set of steel drums. Before long they were filling the inner harbor with tropical songs that sounded perfect with the steel drums. One of them could sing Bob Marley so well it sounded like a recording of the original. When they started playing the classic "Stir It Up," Essie and I began dancing on deck. She pulled me close and whispered to me, "Cappy, did you ever dream in your wildest imagination that we could be here doing this so quickly after so many things went wrong for us?"

"To tell you the truth, Essie, no. I wouldn't have thought it possible in any way."

"I've told you a dozen times. You have to believe that things work out the way they're supposed to. We all have some good and some bad in our lives but, for me, I just have to believe that I'm heading in the right direction and it's all going to work out. And almost always it works out even better than I could have even hoped for even if it doesn't seem possible at the time."

"I love you, Miss Essie."

"Excuse me, that's Mrs. Essie."

"Yes, ma'am."

The inner harbor of Miami was beyond description. There were so many ornate mansions, each one more amazing than the last one you saw. In the back yards, on private docks, were more yachts over a hundred feet than I'd ever seen. Still, Frank's place seemed to be the pick of the litter. And *Buckeye* was definitely the most beautiful yacht in Miami. We eased along into the bay. It was a calm, starlit night. The captain moved *Buckeye* at just the right speed to keep a light breeze moving so insects wouldn't join us for the festivities. The band played one great song after another. Essie and I danced with each other and took a turn with everyone else's significant other throughout the night. I told Frank that this was the most superb dance floor I'd ever been on.

He smiled and explained why it was there. "Les, this is actually a landing pad for my helicopter. We normally bring it with us in case I have to rush out somewhere or we run out of something onboard. We left it in the back yard tonight so we could come out here and party with you all. Pretty good space, eh?"

"Unbelievable. Thank you so much for all of this, Uncle Frank. We are very excited about seeing *Last Dance* tomorrow. I have to tell you that I feel embarrassed that you have paid to have the work done. We could never repay you."

Essie echoed my thoughts, "Uncle Frank, look. We don't have money and you probably wouldn't take it if we did, but I just wanted you to know if there's anything we can do for you, you just name it. You know I can't muscle anybody or anything like that, but 'most anything else."

Frank exploded in a barrel laugh. "Don't you worry about that, sweet Essie. Uncle Frank wouldn't harm a fly and I'd never ask you to do it for me. Muscle someone, now that's funny. And look, your boat didn't cost me a penny. So don't give it a second thought."

"The yard didn't charge you anything?"

"There was a bill. In fact, it was a very expensive bill.

However, you remember my good friend Sylvester that you met earlier this week?"

Uncle Frank and Vinny - almost "family"

"He's the guy who had Vinny tossed in the drink, right?"

"The same. Apparently, he felt so bad about that and, because of some distant connection between the people who 'borrowed' your boat and those he imports through, he felt like paying for your repairs. It was the very least he could do, and he was pleased to pay for a few little options that your boat truly needed."

"Options?"

"Yes, like a new autopilot, radar, refrigeration, GPS, new central heat and air. You know, the things all women want you to have on the boat. I thanked Sylvester for you as I knew you would want me to. He was very happy to do it."

Essie beamed. "Uncle Frank, you are the best relative I've ever had. Not just because you've done a lot for us, but just because, well, just because you are such a cool guy."

"Essie, coming from you, that's as good a compliment as I could ever hope for. It's been my pleasure to help you both. I hope when you get the time, after you finally take your long-awaited cruise, that you'll both come back and visit with Gayle and me again. Maybe even come to our place in Ohio. It's not like this, but it's still a really nice place to pass the time."

"I can only imagine. Don't you worry about it. You'll probably get tired of us before it's over."

"I doubt that. Now let's enjoy this beautiful night."

We all danced on through the evening. As we came back to the dock I'm sure we woke up a lot of Frank's neighbors with our group sing-along of "Margaritaville." But no one complained and I'm sure they never will.

The next day we piled into the chopper and headed to the boat yard. They must be a yard used to dealing with a lot of heavy hitters as it was the only boatyard I'd ever been to that had its own helicopter landing pad. All around were mega yachts similar to *Buckeye*. Essie and I strained looking for *Last Dance*. The yard manager came over and fawned all over Frank and Gayle. They were used to the top drawer treatment and probably expected it. The money it would cost for work at this yard had to be significant.

We walked down to the docks. Essie and I both continued to look for our boat to no avail. In our marina back home, *Last Dance* was one of the larger boats and would be hard to miss. At this yard, our boat would look like a toy. We walked out on one of the large piers and there, nestled between two huge power yachts, was *Last Dance*. To see her took our breath away. It was apparent that they had not stopped on restoring the interior. The rigging had all been replaced as had all the canvas. Even the sails and old winches had been replaced. To top it all off, she had been completely repainted. Essie actually teared up which she didn't even do at our wedding.

We hopped aboard and went below. There was no doubt that she hadn't looked this good the day she was completed at the factory, brand new. All the cabinets had been replaced with the best woods; the lights, upholstery, sinks, stove, everything was new and the very finest quality that could be bought. The varnished bright work looked fifty coats deep. It took my breath away. There was no circumstance that would have ever allowed Essie and me to have a boat this nice.

"So, kids, what do you think?"

"She's beautiful. No doubt she's better than when Gulfstar built her. Everything looks custom."

"It is. I told the yard to fix it back the best it could be done. I didn't want Sylvester to think we had made him look cheap. I was sure he would want you to have the best. And look guys, I hope this doesn't embarrass you, but Dave Pfefferkorn told us you had a little note on her, a personal loan from the guy you bought her from. It's no fun to have that hanging over your head while you're trying to cruise, so Vinny, Tank, Marty, and the rest of the boys paid that off for you. They wanted to help out on the yard bill as a wedding present, but with Sylvester taking care of that, this seemed like the next best thing. So, here she is. She sure looks good to me."

"Frank, we are absolutely speechless. For us, this is like winning the lottery. There's no way we can thank any of you enough."

"Remember, the best thing you can do for any of us is look out for your friends like we tried to do for you. That's a very important, often overlooked concept. It can turn your entire life around."

"Frank, please tell all the guys how grateful we are and that we want to thank them in person."

"I'm sure you'll see them again soon. 'Til then, send them a postcard from the Bahamas."

"I can't wait to take her out. Are they done with her?"

The yard manager was listening and responded. "All she lacks is putting the name back on her. The letters she had were old, out of style. We thought you might like to pick out a new style. For that matter, you could rename her if you wanted. Other than that, any time you're ready for her. Give us thirty minutes notice and we'll help you get underway."

"We have to go back to North Carolina and tie up a couple of things and then we'll be right back. How about having her ready to go next week, like Tuesday or Wednesday."

"She'll be ready. We'll even fuel her up and top off the water tanks. You should be ready to go anywhere you want."

"We can't wait. Let us think on the name and we'll see you next week."

14

Frank and Gayle had been a Godsend to us. Who would have thought that fishing a guy out of the water would ever wind up being such a big part of our lives? We spent one last night at Frank's and told them goodbye early the next day. Frank and Gayle would not be riding back with us as Frank had some business issues come up and he was taking another jet to a resort in Biloxi. We never even bothered to ask what jet he would be using, as we could already imagine.

One of Frank's staff pulled a large van up in front of the house and picked up Essie and me, Jim, Sara, David, Leigh, Tom, and Karen. He drove us to the airport and made sure we were all comfortable on Frank's jet. Two hours later we landed in New Bern and returned to our real world lives. I doubted we would ever have another week like that, but it was very interesting to see how the other half lived.

"We're home, Essie. Just pretend it was all a dream 'cause I doubt you'll ever stay somewhere like that again."

"Don't be so quick to say that, mister. I'm counting on you to make our fortune."

"If being loved is your fortune, you got it. If it's a lot of money, I'm afraid someone has misled you. If I'm anything, I'm the poster child for anti-money. Every time I get close to it, it disappears. But

I do have enough to buy us a chicken wrap at Ratty's. What say we all head over there for a bite?"

Everyone begged off from exhaustion except Jim and Sara. He seemed to have an inexhaustible source of energy, if a good time was involved. We got a table, some sandwiches, and a pitcher of beer. For two hours we recalled the time we had just spent in Miami. Jim and Sara were as in awe of it all just as we were. Jim gave us a ride back to Helen's house. We would pack our bags in the morning and start heading back to the boat as soon as possible.

The drive back to the boat seemed to take forever. Compared to Frank's jet, anyway. We checked in late and spent the night getting used to all the new additions to the boat. When we finally turned in, it felt tremendous to be back in the comfortable berth in our aft cabin. We cut the new air conditioning on as well as a small twelve volt fan over the bed. It couldn't have been any sweeter.

Essie snuggled up next to me. "Cappy, we're finally home and on our way again. Hey, I have a thought on the name. We need to have it put on the stern and bow before we leave anyway."

"Okay, what are you thinking? You tired of *Last Dance*?"

"*Last Dance* was right for where we were back when we got her. But I have a better name and one I think is a lot more positive sounding. *Last Dance* sounds kinda final."

"Okay, lay it on me."

"I'm thinking *Two Peas* like two peas in a pod. That's pretty much who we are. And we name our dinghy 'The Pod.' What do you think?"

"Very nice. I like it. We'll have them put it on in the morning. You know, there is a formal renaming ceremony that tradition and nautical folklore require us to follow. I think it involves some champagne and a virgin."

"The booze is possible but I don't think there are any virgin stores in Florida. What will we do?"

"Let's think about it on the way to the Bahamas and we'll have the ceremony there. Sounds good. Goodnight, my love."

"Good night, Miss Essie."

After a heavy night's sleep, we woke up still in the boatyard. Essie picked out a lettering style for the boat yard and they had the name on her by lunchtime. She picked a dark blue letter with grey drop shadows that made it look almost 3-D in effect. The dock manager came by to inform us that he had just picked us up a new inflatable dinghy to replace the one that had saved our lives but given up its own in the process. We would certainly need one when we got to the Bahamas. He secured it to the new davits on the stern and mounted a small four-stroke outboard on our stern rail. These were things we would never be able to buy on our own. *Thank you, Sylvester. You're a prince.*

We determined to get underway at 4 p.m. so that we would arrive in the Bahamas around noon the next day with the sun directly overhead. That way we could see any coral heads just under the surface. After all this work on the boat, the last thing we needed was to strike something with her. I didn't even want to think about that.

We took an afternoon nap so we would be rested for the long night crossing but I didn't sleep well. The apprehension of an ocean crossing had my adrenalin pumping and had me too wound up to rest. By three thirty I had the diesel running. I heard Essie rattling around in the galley and shortly thereafter I could smell fresh coffee brewing. This was one of those moments on a boat I always lived for, the few minutes before heading out, when you check all the little details and have a cup of coffee. After the check was complete, Essie and I sat down on the new padded cockpit seat cushions and enjoyed our caffeine fix.

"Cappy, this is it. We're finally going to make it to paradise. We'll be there tomorrow afternoon. Goes to show we can do anything we set our minds to."

"I would have given up a long time ago if it weren't for you, Essie. You are my inspiration. I can't tell you how excited I am. You ready to cast off the lines?"

"I am. Let's do it."

"I looked over at the chart on the GPS and got a visual of where we needed to head. I hit the zoom button on the display and looked at a very clear channel on the screen. It was well marked with plenty of water.

"I'm going to have to get used to all this fancy new electronic gear. I'm used to a compass and radio and that's it. With all this high tech stuff, I think *Two Peas* could make the trip without us."

The breeze was light and out of the southwest, the prevailing direction for summertime in this area of the world. Anything out of the north would be bad. This would be perfect. Even a little bit stronger would be good. Within an hour we were clear of land. We passed the number one channel marker on our starboard side and we were in the ocean. The breeze strengthened a little as is to be expected when you get away from obstructions on shore. We had about twelve knots on our starboard and a broad reach that should hold all the way across. We let out all our sail and *Two Peas* responded immediately. She lay over on her port side and jumped to six and half knots of boat speed. I killed the engine and we were moving under sail only. The water made that wonderful sound as it went under us, gently lapping the hull.

Essie put a Luis Miguel CD in the stereo and came to the cockpit with a soft drink and a sandwich. I engaged the autopilot and was delighted to see *Two Peas* follow a straight course with no one having to steer her. We leaned back, relaxed, enjoying the ride, sharing the moment and listening to Luis. Life was too good to hope for. We passed a few fishing boats as we got out into the Gulfstream. The water was a distinctively darker blue and the temperature increase against the hull was quickly apparent. The GPS showed us picking up considerable speed, which impacted our course as we were moving sideways almost as fast as we were moving forward. We could not have had a better day for the crossing.

By ten a.m. we could see land off in the distance. The water under us turned into an aqua blue color and the ocean bottom became visible everywhere. We had made it to the Bahamas Banks. Essie would stay on the bow and try to look out for coral heads as I steered toward shore. We were going to check in at Port Lucaya.

At one p.m. we had tied up in the port and had cleared customs. We wandered around town for several hours enjoying the Bahamian flavor and wound up having dinner in a little joint called Fat Man's Nephew located on the second floor above Fat Man's which was a bar. We both had the conch and some fries. We wanted to eat some of the local food but we couldn't afford to do a lot of restaurant dining. I enjoyed eating on the boat as much as Essie liked to cook. We would be anchoring out a lot and spending as little money at marinas and ashore as possible. Every dollar we spent brought our trip to its conclusion that much sooner. The more frugal we were, the longer we could stay. We were hoping to be there for at least three months.

The next morning we set off for Hope Town, a scenic little harbor town famous for its red and white striped lighthouse and beautiful waters. We motor sailed due to very light winds and cleared Little Abaco by two in the afternoon. We anchored for lunch in a quiet cay and celebrated our arrival with a swim in the crystal clear water. Essie looked around as she put on her swim fins and mask. "They don't have barracudas here, do they?"

"Never. The Bahamas are famous for not having any barracudas or sharks. All you're going to see are little tropical fish. They'll be brightly colored and very friendly."

I was bold in my lie to her because I didn't want her afraid to get in the water. We would be snorkeling every day over here, if I had my way. As luck would have it, my lie was discovered less than two minutes into the swim as Essie practically swam up to a nice specimen of a barracuda. He was only a two-footer but his jaw profile and sharp teeth protruding through it were unmistakable. Essie looked at me and pointed up. We went to the surface and she explained to me how unhappy she was with my fib no matter how worthy the cause. I told her I'd hold her hand as we snorkeled and if she wanted to get out we would. She decided to give it a try and we snorkeled for a full hour. The well-toothed fish remained with us almost the entire time as if he were watching a silent film starring us. I felt this would not be a good time to mention to Essie the six-foot grey reef shark I saw in the distance the entire time we were in the water that day. We finally got back in the cockpit, dried off, and Essie fixed us some lunch.

The entrance to Hope Town harbor was beautiful. The famous lighthouse was easily seen as you entered. It had been worth all the trouble to get there. We both marveled at how spectacular the place was. We found an empty corner of the harbor and dropped anchor. I backed down on the chain until I was certain we were secure and killed the motor. Essie came over to me and practically jumped into my arms.

"Cappy, we did it. We're here. We finally got to heaven. I want to enjoy and appreciate every second we're here. I want to see everything and experience every foot of it. It's so beautiful. We did it."

"I know. It's been a hell of an adventure but we're finally here. I'm with you. I want to rest, enjoy, and savor all the secluded, quiet little harbors the Bahamas have to offer. We can always party with friends when we get back home. But not here. This is going to be the respite of a lifetime."

About thirty minutes after we dropped the hook, we heard a small plane engine. It buzzed low and circled the harbor looking for a level place to land. Sure enough, on the next pass it centered itself just outside the entrance to the harbor and landed on its pontoons. It taxied into the harbor and dropped an anchor of its own about a hundred yards away from us. A familiar voice called to us as he stepped out of the cockpit and onto the pontoon. It was Grimshaw.

"Ahoy, *Two Peas*, got any room for friends for dinner?" Behind him we could see Sara, small bag in hand. I looked at Essie and she was the first to respond. "Get your butts over here. Drinks on the lido deck in ten minutes."

I could say that the evening ended that way, but that wouldn't be the full story. Just before dark, we heard the blare of a horn and turned to see an extremely large vessel entering the harbor. It had a familiar silhouette. As it made the final turn and dropped its own anchor, we could clearly read the name in back-lighted stainless steel across the side of the main cabin. It was *Katz Meow*. We were too tired to go calling that evening but we certainly would be taking the dinghy over to visit in the morning. Even Grimshaw, after four beers said, "Cappy, that looks a lot like Melinda's boat, doesn't it?"

"You guessed it, Jim. This is going to be interesting, I'm sure."

I don't know how or why we thought the Bahamas were going to be some remote anchorage where we would do nothing but swim and sleep. Perhaps we'd have to sail to some atoll in the South Pacific? To think about it, why would we want to be away from everybody we loved? Paradise is best enjoyed when it's shared.

Jim and Sara

That night as we lay in our aft berth, Jim and Sara in the V-berth, Essie and I reminisced about all that had gone on in our lives over the past two years. We had loved every minute of it.

We couldn't picture ourselves in some nine-to-five job and land-bound ever again. We kissed and said goodnight. After a few minutes, Essie pulled over close to me and whispered, "Cappy, can I ask you a serious question?"

"Of course you can. What's on your mind?"

"This is just hypothetical, of course. What do you suppose it would be like, raising a couple of kids on a sailboat?

The End, for now…

**If you don't have a dream,
you can't have a dream come true.**

Two Peas **sailing on the Neuse River**

About the Author

Les Pendleton lives in historic New Bern, North Carolina. His writing style conveys the influence of his career in motion pictures. Many people share their impression that reading his novels feels as if you are watching the characters come to life on the silver screen. Actual locations in coastal North Carolina are featured in many of his books. His writing spans a wide array of genres from action adventure, romance, historical fiction, suspense-filled mysteries and autobiographies. Les spends every free moment with his family and friends sailing in Pamlico Sound and the Atlantic Coast.

For more about the author, visit **www.lespendleton.com**

* * *

Thank you for reading this novel.
We invite you to share your thoughts and reactions
by going to Amazon.com/author/lespendleton
and posting a review.

Essie Press

48235628R00137

Made in the USA
Middletown, DE
13 September 2017